Adam to Muhammad

Abdul Waheed

Adam to Muhammad

Abdul Waheed

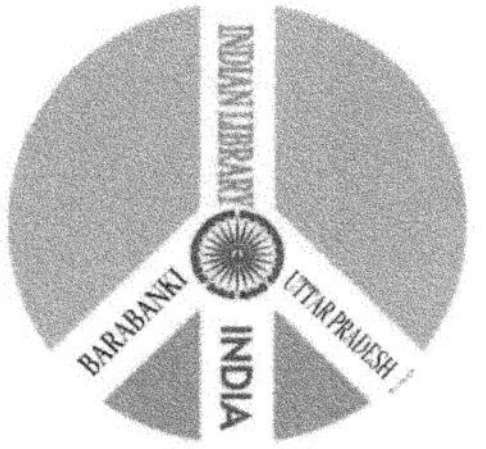

INDIAN LIBRARY
BARABANKI
UTTAR PRADESH
INDIA

Dedication

This book is dedicated to the memory of my late father Haji Ubairdur Rahman (Munna) and younger brother Abdul Hameed. May God (Allah) give peace to his soul. Aameen

Table content

Preface

There are stories about all the prophets or messengers who came from Adam to Mohammed, that is, from Hazrat Adam Alaihissalam to Muhammad Rasoolullah, those stories are mentioned in the Holy Quran and the Bible and are also mentioned under some other names in many religions of the world.

This small book contains a brief sequential description about him. My effort has been to collect as much information as possible about these Ambiya, but I have given as much information as I can. If you have any more information than that, please let me know. I will try to share your information,

Thank you.

Abdul Waheed, Barabanki, Uttar Pradesh, India

Adam

Adam is the name given to the first human in Genesis 1–5. In addition to its use as the name of the first man, the Bible also uses Adam as a pronoun, personally as "a human being", and in the collective sense. Genesis 1 tells of God's creation of the world and its creatures, including Adam, meaning the human race; In Genesis 2 God creates "Adam", this time meaning a single male human, from the "dust of the ground", places him in the Garden of Eden, and makes a woman, Eve, as his companion; In Genesis 3 Adam and Eve ate from the Tree of Knowledge and God condemned Adam to toil on the earth for food and return at his death; Genesis 4 relates the birth of Adam's sons, and Genesis 5 lists his descendants from Seth to Noah.

In the entire Hebrew Bible, Adam appears only in chapters 1–5 of the Book of Genesis, with the exception of one mention at the beginning of the Books of Chronicles, where, as in Genesis, he tops the list of Israel's ancestors. The majority view among scholars is that the final text of Genesis dates to the Persian period (5th century BCE), but all other characters and events mentioned in Genesis chapters 1–11 are absent from the rest. The Hebrew Bible has led a large minority to conclude that these chapters were composed much later than the chapters that follow, possibly in the 3rd century BCE.

in the Hebrew Bible

Genesis 1 tells of God's creation of the world and its creatures, with the human race being his final creation: "He created them male and female, and blessed them, and called their names Adam..." (Genesis 5 :2). God blesses mankind, commands them to "be fruitful and increase in number," and gives them "dominion over the fish of the sea, over the birds of the air, over the livestock, over all the earth, and over every creeping thing that moves." creeping upon the earth" (Genesis 1.26-27).

In Genesis 2, God created "Adam", this time meaning a single male human, from "the dust of the ground", and "breathed into his nostrils the breath of life" (Genesis 2:7). Then God placed this first man in the Garden of Eden, and said to him, "You may freely eat from every tree in the garden; but you must never eat from the tree of the knowledge of good and evil." :For if you eat any of it during the day, you will surely die" (Genesis 2:16-17). God says that "it is not good that the man should be alone"

Post-biblical Jewish traditions

Adam, Lucas Cranach the Elder
God himself took dust from the four corners of the earth, and created Adam from each color (red for blood, black for intestines, white for bones and sinews, and green for pale skin). The soul of Adam is the image of God, and just as God fills the world, so the Spirit fills the human body: "Just as God sees all things, and is visible to no one, so the Spirit sees, but is not seen As God guides the world, so the spirit guides the body; as God is pure in his holiness, so is the soul; and as God dwells in secret, so is the spirit."Jewish According to the literature, Adam had a body of light, similar to the light created by God on the first day, and Adam's original glory could be recovered through mystical contemplation of God.
Adam, Lilith and Eve

The rabbis, puzzled by the fact that Genesis 1 states that God created man and woman together, while Genesis 2 describes them being created separately, pointed out that when God created Adam So they also created a woman from clay, just as they had created

Adam, and named her. Lilith; But the two could not agree, because Adam wanted Lilith to lie beneath him, and Lilith insisted that Adam lie beneath her, and so she ran away from him, and Eve was created from Adam's rib. His story was significantly developed during the Middle Ages, in the tradition of Aggadic Midrashim, the Zohar, and Jewish mysticism. Other rabbis interpreted the same verse to mean that Adam was created as a being with two faces, male and female, or as a single hermaphroditic being, male and female joined one after the other, but God saw that walking from And it became difficult to negotiate, and hence divided them. apart.

Eve's mistake in the fall

The serpent came to Eve instead of Adam because Adam had heard God's Word with his own ears, while Eve had only his report; Eve tasted the fruit and immediately knew that she was doomed to death, and she said to herself that it would be better if she tricked Adam into eating it so that he too would die, and not be replaced by another woman. Adam ate the fruit, unaware of what he was doing, and was filled with sorrow. When Adam blamed Eve after eating the forbidden fruit, God rebuked her saying that as a man Adam should not have obeyed his wife, because she is the head, not he.

Adam and the winter solstice

An aggadic legend found in tractate Avodah Zarah 8a contains comments about the Roman mid-winter holidays and the Talmudic hypothesis that Adam first established the tradition of fasting before the winter solstice and rejoicing thereafter, The festival later evolved into the Roman Saturnalia and Calenda.

children of adam and eve

Adam is separated from Eve for 130 years.

in Christian

The idea of original sin is found neither in Judaism nor in Islam, and was introduced into Christianity by the Apostle Paul, based on currents of Hellenistic Jewish thought that held that Adam's sin created the world. I had introduced death and sin. Sin, for Paul, was a power to which all men are subject, but the coming of Christ provided the means by which the righteous would be restored to the paradise from which Adam's sin had exiled the human race. They did not imagine that this original sin of Adam would be transmitted biologically or that subsequent generations would be punished for the actions of a distant ancestor. It was Augustine who took this step by locating sin in the male semen: when Adam and Eve ate the fruit they were ashamed and covered their private parts, identifying the place from which the first sin passed on to all future generations. Was passed in. Only Jesus Christ, who was not conceived by human semen, was free from the taint passed on from Adam. (Augustine's idea was based on the ancient world's ideas on biology, according to which male sperm contained the entire unborn baby, the mother's womb being no more than a nurturing chamber in which it grew.)

in islam

In Islam, God created Adam (Arabic: آدم) from handfuls of soil taken from all over the world, which explains why people around the world have different skin colors. According to the Islamic creation myth, he was the first prophet of Islam and the first Muslim. The Quran says that all the prophets preached faith equal to devotion to God. When God informed the angels that He would create a vice-ruler (a Caliph) on earth, the angels inquired, "Will You place there people who will spread corruption and bloodshed?" So God showed himself to the angels and said, "Tell me their names?" The angels had no knowledge of these, because God had not taught them. Then God allowed Adam to reveal these names to them, and said, "Did I not tell you (the angels) that I know what is invisible in the heavens and the earth, and that I know that you (the angels) What do you reveal and what do you (Satan) conceal;"
the scholar Al-Tabari explained that God was referring to Iblis (Satan) of his evil plans and to the angels of their honesty.

in Mandeism

In Mandaism, Adam is considered the founder and first prophet of the religion. He initiates the true path of Manda (knowledge) and enlightenment. He is seen as a leper or preacher of divine truth. 31,45 According to the Mandaean calendar, 2021-2022 CE will correspond to the Mandaean year 445391 AA (AA = after the creation of Adam) in the Gregorian calendar.

in Gnostic ideology

In the ancient Gnostic text on the origin of the world, Adam originally appears as a primordial being born from the light emanating from the Aeon known as Forebode. Accordingly, his primordial form is called Adam of Light. But when he wished to reach the Eighth Heaven, he was unable to do so due to the corruption in his light. Thus he creates his own realm, consisting of six universes and their worlds which are seven times superior to the Heaven of Chaos. All of these realms exist in the area between the Eighth Heaven and the chaos below it. But when the archers saw him, they realized that the chief creator of the material world (Yaldabaoth) had lied to them by claiming that he was the only god. However, they decide to create a physical version of Adam in the image of the spiritual Adam. But Sophia later sends her daughter Zoe (spiritual Eve) to give life to physical Adam before physical Eve leaves with Adam and enters the Tree of Knowledge. However, according to the Hypostasis of the Archons, a spirit descends on the physical Adam and gives him a living soul.

in the Druze faith

The Druze consider Adam to be the first spokesman (natiq), who helped convey the fundamental teachings of monotheism (tawhid) to a larger audience. He is also considered an important prophet of God in the Druze faith, being one of seven prophets who appeared in different periods of history.

In other religions and unconventional practices

Some Taoists of the Tang dynasty, inspired by Emperor Taizong's syncretic beliefs and the policies that encouraged it, viewed the Christian version of Jesus as a redemptive expression of "The Way", and also revered their ancestors, including Adam.

Some Mongolian Christians and Muslims thought that Adam was the same person as Gautama Buddha.

historical

While a traditional view was that the book of Genesis was written by Moses and considered it historical and allegorical, modern scholars consider the Genesis creation narrative to be one of various ancient origin myths.

Analysis such as the documentary hypothesis also suggests that the text is the result of a compilation of several previous traditions, explaining the apparent contradictions. Other stories from the same canonical book, such as the Genesis flood narrative, are also thought to have been influenced by older literature.

Asr al-Tafsir's interpretation of the words of Abu Bakr al-Jaza'iri.

7 Al-Araf 19

Abu Bakr al-Jazairi (born 1921 AD) (died 2018 AD)
Word Explanation:
And your wife: she is Eve, whom Almighty God created from the left rib of Adam.

Heaven: The Abode of Peace where the Messenger of God, may God bless him and grant him peace, entered the Night of Night Journey and Mi'raj.

Of the wrongdoers: i.e. for themselves.

Whispers: The hidden voice, and whispering of Satan to the son of Adam, putting into his breast corrupt and hurtful meanings which make it beautiful for him to believe, say, or do.

To reveal to them what is hidden: to show them what is hidden in their faults.
And he divided them; He made each of them take an oath.

So he brought them down by deceit, that is, by tricking and deceiving them, he gradually brought them down until they ate the fruit from the tree.

And they began to cover themselves, and they tied the leaves of paradise around themselves to cover their private parts.

Meaning of the verse:
When the Most Merciful expelled Satan from Paradise, he called Adam, saying to him: "And Adam, you and your wife," meaning Eve, "dwell in Paradise, so eat wherever you wish," meaning from its fruits and good things, "and do not come near this thing." Jarrah" He pointed to a specific tree of Paradise and forbade them from eating from it. He taught them that if they ate from it, they would be wrongdoers deserving of punishment, and Satan took advantage of this opportunity that was given to him by whispering to them, making it attractive for them to eat from the tree, saying to them: {Your Lord has not forbidden you from this tree except that you become angels or that you become of something else. The debt {and he divided it between them} that is, he swore to them that he would He advised them and not a fraud for them, {so they made them with vanity} and deceived until they were eaten {so when the tree was lost, it started ...} that is, they appeared to them, whether they were the light that was covered by them, so they made them tightened from the paper of heaven to themselves, and it is the meaning of their nakedness, On them are the leaves of Paradise. Then their Lord, Glory be to Him, called them, saying: Did I not forbid you from this tree? It is an

interrogative of correction and reprimand, {And I say to you that Satan is your clear enemy.} So how did you accept his advice while he was your enemy?

Guidance of the verses
1- Satan's weapon with which he fights the son of Adam is whispering and embellishment and nothing else.

2- Reporting Satan's enmity toward man.
3- The prohibition requires prohibition unless there is evidence that diverts it from being disliked.

4- It is obligatory for both men and women to cover their private parts.

5- It is permissible to swear by God Almighty, but only one who is truthful should swear.
Tafsir Ibn Kathir

Surah: 7. Al-Araaf -Verse: 19

O Adam, settle you and your wife in the Garden, then eat from it wherever you please, but do not go near this tree, lest you become one of the wrongdoers.

Almighty God has mentioned that He permitted Adam, peace be upon him, and his wife Eve, from Paradise, to eat from all but one tree and eat all its fruits. This has been discussed earlier in Surat Al-Baqarah.

Enoch (Idris)

Idris is an ancient prophet mentioned in the Quran, whom Muslims believe was the third prophet after Seth. He is the second prophet mentioned in the Quran. Islamic tradition has unanimously identified Idris with the Biblical Enoch, although many Muslim scholars of the classical and medieval periods also held that Idris and Hermes Trismegistus were the same person. [contradictory]

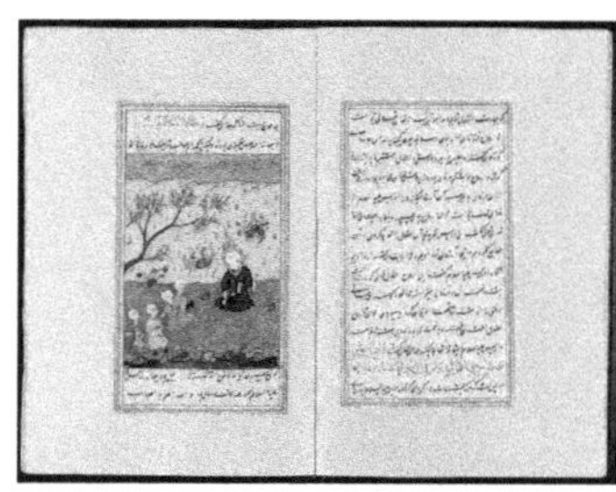

The Quran describes him as "trustworthy" and "patient" and the Quran also says that he was "raised to a high position". Because of this and other similarities, Idris has traditionally been identified with the Biblical Enoch, and Islamic tradition generally places Idris in the early generations of Adam, and considers him one of the oldest prophets mentioned in the Quran, Keeps him between Adam. And Noah. Idris's unique status inspired many future traditions and stories surrounding him in Islamic folklore.

According to the hadith, narrated by Malik ibn Anas and found in Sahih Muslim, it is said that on Muhammad's night journey, he encountered Idris in the fourth heaven. The traditions that developed around the character of Idris have given him the scope of a prophet as well as a philosopher and mystic, and several later Muslim mystics, or Sufis, including Ruzbihan Bakali and Ibn Arabi, also encountered Idris. Mentioned to do. In his spiritual philosophy.

Idris is generally considered to be identical with the patriarch Enoch who lived in the generations from Adam. Several Quran commentators, such as al-Tabari and Qadi Badawi, identified Idris with Enoch. Baijawi said, "Idris was the son of Seth and the ancestor of Noah, and his name was Enoch (Ar. Akhnukh)". Barsali Ismail Haqqi's commentary on the Fushu al-Aiqam by Ibn Arabi.

Idris is mentioned twice in the Quran, where he is described as a wise man.

In Sura 19 of the Quran, Maryam, God says:
Also mention the case of Idris in the book: He was a truthful (and honest) man, (and) a prophet:

And We raised him to a high place.

—Quran 19:56–57 (Yusuf Ali)

Later, in Sura 21, al-Anbiya, Idris is praised again:

And (remember) Ismail, Idris, and Dhu al-Kifl, all (men) of steadfastness and patience;

We included them in Our mercy, for they were among the righteous.

—Quran 21:85–86 (Yusuf Ali)

Noah (Nuh)

Noah's story appears in the Hebrew Bible (Book of Genesis, chapters 5-9), the Quran, and the Bahá'í writings. Noah is mentioned in various other books of the Bible, including the New Testament and related deuterocanonical books.

Major pilgrimage

On a hill in Karak, Lebanon

The Genesis flood story is one of the most famous stories in the Bible. In this account, Noah worked faithfully to build the ark at God's command, and ultimately saved not only his family, but the human race and all land animals from extinction during the Flood, which God repented of. Was that the world was full of sin. Later, God made a covenant with Noah and promised that He would never again destroy all living beings on the earth with a flood. Noah is also depicted as a "tiller of the soil" and a drinker of wine. After the Flood, God commanded Noah and his sons to "be fruitful and increase in number, and replenish the earth".

A Jewish depiction of Noah

Noah's righteousness is a matter of much discussion among rabbis. The description of Noah as "righteous in his generation" implies to some that his perfection was only relative: in his generation of wicked people, he might have been considered righteous, but in the generation of tzaddiks like Abraham, he would not have been. Will be considered. Righteous. They point out that Noah did not pray to God for the people who were about to be destroyed, as Abraham prayed for the wicked of Sodom and Gomorrah. In fact, Noah is never seen speaking; He simply listens to God and acts on His orders. This has led some commentators to posit the image of Noah as "the righteous man in the fur coat" who ensured his own comfort while neglecting his neighbor's. Others, such as the medieval commentator Rashi, believed to the contrary, that the building of the Ark was deliberately prolonged by 120 years to give sinners time to repent. Rashi interpreted his father's statement about naming...

2 Peter 2:5 refers to Noah as "a preacher of righteousness." In the Gospel of Matthew and the Gospel of Luke, Jesus compares Noah's flood to the coming Day of Judgment: "As it was in the days of Noah, so it will be in the days of the coming of the Son of man. For before the flood In those days, people were eating and drinking, marrying and giving in marriage, until the day that Noah entered into the ark; and they did not know until the flood came and took them all away, It will happen at the coming of the Son of man."
The First Epistle of Peter compares the power of baptism to the ark saving those who were in it. In later Christian thought, the Ark came to be compared to the Church: salvation was to be found only within Jesus Christ and His Lordship, just as in Noah's time it was found only within the Ark. St. Augustine of Hippo (354-430), in The City of God, demonstrated that the dimensions of the arch correspond to the dimensions of the human body...

according to the bible

The tenth and last of the pre-Flood (antediluvian) patriarchs, the son of Lamech and an unnamed mother, Noah lived 500 years before the birth of his sons Shem, Ham, and Japheth.

genesis flood story

The story of the Genesis flood is contained in the Bible in chapters 6-9 of the Book of Genesis. The narrative indicates that God intended to return the Earth to its pre-creation water-chaos state by causing a flood due to humanity's misdeeds and then reconstructing it using the microcosm of Noah's ark. . Thus, the flood was not a simple overflow but a reversal of creation. The narrative discusses the evil of mankind that led God to destroy the world through a flood, certain animals, the preparation of the ark for Noah and his family, and God's guarantee for the continued existence of life (Noah Covenant of) discussed. The promise that He would never send another flood.
after the flood

After the flood, Noah offered burnt offerings to God. God accepted the sacrifice, and made a covenant with Noah, and through him with all mankind, that He would not destroy the earth or destroy man with another flood.

"And God blessed Noah and his sons, and said to them, Be fruitful and increase in number, and fill the earth" The rainbow was set in the clouds as a pledge of this merciful covenant with man and beast Was (ib. viii. 15-22, ix. 8-17). Two injunctions were imposed on Noah: while eating animal food was permitted, abstinence from blood was strictly prohibited; and the shedding of blood by man by man was made a crime punishable by death (ib. ix. 3–6).

Noah, as the last of the extremely long-lived antediluvian patriarchs, died 350 years after the flood, at the age of 950, when Terah was 128 years old. As depicted in the Bible, the maximum human life span gradually decreased thereafter, from about 1,000 years to Moses' 120 years.
After the flood, the Bible says that Noah became a farmer and planted a vineyard. He drank the wine of this vineyard and became drunk; And remained lying "open" inside

his tent. Noah's son Ham, father of Canaan, saw his father naked and told his brothers, causing Ham's son Canaan to be cursed by Noah.

At the beginning of the Classical era, commentators on Genesis 9:20–21 condoned Noah's excessive drinking because he was considered the first drinker; First person to discover the effects of alcohol. John Chrysostom, Archbishop of Constantinople and a Church Father, wrote in the fourth century that Noah's behavior is defensible: as the first human to taste wine, he would not have known its effects: "Ignorance of the proper quantity of drinking and Due to inexperience, got drunk". Philo, a Hellenistic Jewish philosopher, also forgave Noah by saying that one can drink wine in two different ways: Drinking to excess is a sin peculiar to the vicious...

In reference to Noah's drunkenness, two facts are related: (1) Noah became drunk and "he became naked within his tent", and (2) Ham "saw the nakedness of his father, and the nakedness of his two brothers." Told out"
Due to its brevity and textual inconsistencies, it has been suggested that this narrative is "a fragment of a more important story". A complete account would explain what Ham actually did to his father, or why Noah cursed Canaan for Ham's misdeeds, or how Noah realized what had happened. In the field of psychological biblical criticism, J. H. Allens and W. Yes. Rollins has analyzed the unconventional behavior that occurs between Noah and Ham in comparison to other Hebrew Bible texts, such as Habakkuk 2:15, which revolves around sexuality and the display of genitals. and Lamentations 4:21.

Other comments noted that "exposing one's nakedness" can mean having sex with that person or that person's spouse, as in...

Genesis 10 brings forth the descendants of Shem, Ham, and Japheth, whose nations spread across the earth after the Flood. Japheth's descendants were the Sea Nations (10:2-5). Cush, son of Ham, had a son named Nimrod, who became the first mighty man on earth, a mighty hunter, king of Babylon and the land of Shinar (10:6-10). From there Ashur went and settled Nineveh. (10:11-12) The descendants of Canaan – the Sidonians, the Hitthites, the Jebusites, the Amorites, the Girgashites, the Hivites, the Arkites, the Zinites, the Arvadites, the Zemarites, and the Hamathites – spread from Sidon to Gerar. , near Gaza, and as far as Sodom and Gomorrah (10:15-19). Among Shem's descendants was Eber (10:21).

These genealogies are structurally different from the genealogy set forth in Genesis 5 and 11. It has a segmented or tree-like structure, which is passed from one father to many offspring. It is strange that the table, which assumes that the population is distributed around the Earth, is preceded by the account of To...

narrative analysis

According to the documentary hypothesis, the first five books of the Bible (Pentateuch/Torah), including Genesis, were collected during the 5th century BCE from four main sources, which themselves date no earlier than the 10th century BCE. Two of these, the Jahwist, composed in the 10th century BC, and the Priestly source, from the late 7th century BC, form the chapters of Genesis that deal with Noah. An attempt by a 5th-century editor to accommodate two independent and sometimes conflicting sources leads to confusion over such matters as how many of each animal Noah took, and how long the flood lasted.

The Oxford Encyclopedia of the Books of the Bible notes that this story echoes parts of the Garden of Eden story: Noah is the first vintner, while Adam is the first farmer; Both have problems with their produce; Both stories contain nudity; And both involve division between brothers resulting in a curse. However, after the flood, St...

Tafseer

Tafsir Ibn Kathir
Surah: 71. Noah - Verse: 1

Verily, We sent Noah to his people: Warn your people before a painful torment befalls them.

Explanation of Surat Nuh, which is Mecca.

Almighty God tells us about Noah, peace be upon him, that He sent him to his people ordering him to warn them of God's punishment before it came upon them, so that if they repent and If they repent, it will go away from them. That is why he said: "Warn your people before a painful punishment befalls them."

Abraham (Ibrahim)

In Jewish tradition, Abraham is referred to as Avraham Avinu (Абрахᴎ Абино), "Abraham our father", indicating that he is both the biological ancestor of the Jews and the father of Judaism, the first Jew. His story is read in the weekly Torah reading portions, primarily in the parashot: Lech-Lecha (λκ֣־λֵ֥ה), Vayera (أغوري), Chayei Sara (חַיֵּי שָׂרָה), and Toledot (تولדﮦ).

Hanan bar Rava taught in the name of Abba Arikha that Abraham's mother's name was Ămatla'y Bat Karnebo.

 In Jewish legends, God created the heavens and the earth for the sake of Abraham's virtues. After the Biblical flood, Abraham was the only one among the holy people who seriously swore never to leave God, studied in the house of Noah and Shem to learn about "the ways of God", continued the line of High Priest from Noah and Shem, and assigning the office to Levi and his seed forever. Before leaving his father's land, Abraham was miraculously saved from the fiery furnace of Nimrod following his brave action of breaking the idols of the Chaldeans into pieces. During his sojourning in Canaan, Abraham was accustomed to extend hospitality to travelers and strangers and taught how to praise God also knowledge of God to those who had received his kindness.

Along with Isaac and Jacob, he is the person whose name would appear united with God, since in Judaism God is known as Elohi Abraham, Elohi Yitzchak ve Elohi Ya'aqob ("God of Abraham, God of Isaac, and God of Jacob"). Was called. And never anyone else's god. He was also mentioned as the father of thirty nations.

Abraham is generally credited as the author of the Sefer Yetzirah, one of the oldest extant books on Jewish mysticism.

According to Pirkei Avot, Abraham had to undergo ten trials at God's command. The binding of Isaac is referred to in the Bible as a test; The other nine are not specified, but later rabbinical sources give different calculations.

In Christianity, Abraham is revered as the prophet to whom God chose to reveal himself and with whom God initiated a covenant (cf. covenant theology). The Apostle Paul declared that all who believe in Jesus (Christians) "are included in the seed of Abraham and are heirs of the promise made to Abraham." In Romans 4, Abraham is praised for his "unwavering faith" in God. , which is linked to the concept of participants in the covenant of grace "who demonstrate faith in the saving power of Christ".

Throughout history, church leaders, following Paul, have emphasized Abraham as the spiritual father of all Christians. Augustine of Hippo declared that Christians are Abraham's "children (or "seed") by faith, Ambrose said that "through their faith

Christians fulfill the promises made to Abraham", and Martin Luther said Abraham "Remembered as an exemplary man of faith."[e]

The Roman Catholic Church, the largest Christian denomination, calls Abraham "our...".

historical

In the early and mid-20th century, William F. Albright and G. Prominent archaeologists such as Ernest Wright and biblical scholars such as Albrecht Alt and John Bright believed that the patriarchs and matriarchs were either real persons or credible composites of people who lived. "Patriarchal Era", 2nd millennium BC. But, in the 1970s, new arguments related to Israel's past and the Biblical texts challenged these views; This argument was made by Thomas L. Can be found in Thompson's The Historicity of the Patriarchal Narratives (1974), and John Van Seters' Abraham in History and Tradition (1975). Thompson, a literary scholar, based his argument on archeology and ancient texts.

His thesis centered on the lack of compelling evidence that the patriarchs lived in the 2nd millennium BCE, and noted how certain biblical texts reflected first millennium conditions and concerns. Van Seters examined the patriarchal stories and argued that their names, social milieu, and messages strongly suggested that they were Iron Age creations. Van Seter and Thompson's works were a paradigm shift in biblical scholarship and archaeology, which gradually led scholars to no longer consider the patriarchal narratives as historical.] Some conservative scholars attempted to defend the Patriarchal narratives in the following years, but this has not found acceptance among scholars. By the beginning of the 21st century, archaeologists had stopped trying to recover any context that would make Abraham, Isaac or Jacob credible historical figures.

The story of Abraham, like that of the other patriarchs, probably had a substantial oral prehistory (he is mentioned in the Book of Ezekiel and the Book of Isaiah). Like Moses, the name Abraham is apparently very ancient, as the tradition found in the Book of

Genesis no longer understands its original meaning (presumably "the father is great" – the meaning given in Genesis 17:5, "many "the father of the people", is a false etymology). At some stage oral traditions became part of the written tradition of the Pentateuch; Most scholars believe that this phase dates back to the Persian period, approximately

520–320 BCE. The mechanisms by which this came about remain unknown, but there are currently at least two hypotheses. The first, called Persian Imperial authorisation, is that the post-Exilic community devised the Torah as a legal basis on which to function within the Persian Imperial system; the second is that the Pentateuch was written to provide the criteria for determining who would belong to the post-Exilic Jewish community and to establish the power structures and relative positions of its various groups, notably the priesthood and the lay "elders".

The completion of the Torah and its elevation to the center of post-exilic Judaism was about the combination of older texts as well as new writings – the final Pentateuch being based on existing traditions. In the Book of Ezekiel, written during the exile (i.e., in the first half of the 6th century BCE), the Babylonian exile Ezekiel states that those who remained in Judah are claiming ownership of the land by inheritance from Abraham. From; But the prophet told them that they had no claim because they did not follow the Torah. The Book of Isaiah similarly testifies to the tension between the people of Judah and the Jews returning after the exile ("Golah"), stating that God is Israel's father and that Israel's history begins in the Exodus, with Abraham. No. , The conclusion that can be drawn from this and similar evidence (e.g., Ezra–Nehemiah), is that the figure of Abraham must have been preeminent among the great landowners of Judah at the time of the Exile and after, serving to support their claims to the land in opposition to those of the returning exiles.

Tafsir

Tafsir Ibn Kathir

Surah: 2. Al-Baqarah -Verse: 127

And when Abraham raised the foundations of the House, and Ishmael, "Our Lord, accept it from us. Verily, You are the Hearer, the Knower."

For the Almighty says: (And when Abraham laid the foundation of the House and Ishmael, "Our Lord, accept from us. Verily, You are the Hearer, the Knower. Our Lord, and make us submissive to you, and from us a community submissive to you. , and show us our rites, and accept our repentance. Verily, You are the Accepting, the Merciful.)

So base: plural of base, which is pillar and foundation. God Almighty says: And remember, O Muhammad, the building of Abraham and Ishmael for your people, peace be upon them, the House, and they created foundations from it, and they said: (Our Lord, accept from us. Verily (You are the Hearer, the Knower.) So they are in good deeds, and they are asking God Almighty. That it be accepted from them, as Ibn Abi Hatim narrated from the hadith of Muhammad bin Yazid bin Khanis al-Makki on the authority of Wahib bin al-Ward: He said: (And when Abraham laid the foundation of the House and Ishmael, our Lord, accept from us) Then he shouted and said: O Friend of the Most Merciful, raise up the pillars of the House of the Most Merciful. And you're sorry he won't accept...

Asr al-Tafsir's interpretation of the words of Abu Bakr al-Jazairi

6 Al-Anām 78

Abu Bakr al-Jazairi (born 1921 AD) (died 2018 AD)

Word Explanation:

Ibrahim: He is Ibrahim Khalil al-Rahman ibn Azar, one of the sons of Shem ibn Noah, peace be upon him.

Statues: The plural of statue is statues made of stone.

Devta: Plural of Ishwar which means God.

In error: To deviate from the path of truth.

State: State.

Night came upon him, it became dark.

When it disappeared: That is, it disappeared.

Emerging: Emerging and emerging.

Losers: Those who follow the path of truth and follow the path of falsehood.

I directed my face: I turned my heart toward my Lord and turned away from anything. Hanifa: Leaning from error to guidance.

meaning of verse

The context in explaining the guidance to those who are just to their Lord is still idols that they worship in order that they may be guided. Then God Almighty said to His Messenger Muhammad, may God bless him and grant him peace: {And when Abraham said to his father Azar}, meaning, and mention to them the saying of Abraham to Abu Azar: {Do you take idols as gods} meaning, do you make statues of gods from stones? Lords that you and your people worship. {Indeed, I see you}, O my father, {and your people in clear error} through the path of truth whose pursuer is saved and successful. This is what the first verse [74] indicates. As for the second verse [75], God Almighty says: {And thus We show Abraham the kingdom of heaven. And the earth } That is, just as we showed him the right to invalidate his father's worship of idols, we also show him the manifestations of our ability, knowledge, and wisdom that lead to our divinity in the kingdom of the heavens and the earth, so that he will be among those who are certain, and certainty is one of the highest levels of faith. This is what is indicated in the second verse and in the third [76]. God Almighty detailed what is most beautiful in His saying, "We showed Abraham the kingdom of the heavens and the earth," and God Almighty said: "And when the night fell upon him," that is, it became dark, "he saw a star." It may be Al-Zahra {This is my Lord said, but when He said} That is, the star set. {He said, 'No, I love those who descend. Of the misguided people, in knowing their true Lord. {Then when he saw the sun rising} meaning rising {he said: This is my Lord, this is greater} meaning than the planet and the moon {then when it set} meaning it set with the onset of the night {he said, "Arise, I am innocent of what you have done." Shirkun}. Thus, Abraham confronted his people, the worshipers of the stars represented by his carved idols. He confronted them with the truth that he wanted to reach them with them, which is the invalidation of worship other than God Almighty. He said, "Indeed, I have turned my face to Him who created the heavens and the earth, upright." Not as you turn your faces to idols that you protect with your hands and worship. By your desires, not by the command of your Lord, and it was announced His innocence was clear and frank: He said: {And I am not of the polytheists}.

Guidance of the verses

From the guidance of the verses:
1- Denying polytheism against its people, and not approving it, even if they are the closest people to one.

2- God Almighty's grace and favor upon whomever He wills through guidance that leads to its highest levels.

3- The demand for certainty is one of the most honorable and dearest demands, and it is achieved by contemplating and considering the verses.

4- Inferring the existence of the All-Wise Maker, God Almighty, from occurrence.

5- Year of graduation in education.

6- The necessity of disavowing polytheism and its people.
Tafsir al-Qurtubi

Surah: 6. Al-Anam -Verse: 74

And when Abraham said to his father Azar, "Do you take idols as gods?" Indeed, I see you and your people in clear error.

God Almighty said: And when Abraham said to his father Azar: Do you take idols as gods? Indeed, I see that you and your people are in clear error. God Almighty said: And when Abraham said, the scholars spoke about this; Abu Bakr Muhammad ibn Muhammad ibn al-Hasan al-Juwayni al-Shafi'i al-Ash'ari said in his commentary on the jokes: There is no difference among people regarding the name of Abraham's father being Terah. What is indicated in the Qur'an is that his name is Azar. It was said: Azar has a disparagement in their language. It is as if he said: And when he said to his father, O mistaken one, do you take idols as gods? If that is the case, then the choice is nominative. It was said: Azar is the name of an idol. If that is the case, then its position is in the accusative case, indicating the implicit meaning of the verb. It is as if he said: When Abraham said to his father, "Do you take Azar as a god? Do you take idols as gods?" I said: What he claimed of agreement is not based on agreement. Muhammad bin Ishaq, Al-Kalbi, and Al-Dahhak said: Azer Abu Ibrahim, peace be upon him, and he is Terah, are like Israel and Jacob. I said that it has two names, as mentioned above. Muqatil said: Azar is a title, and Terah is a name, and Al-Thaalabi narrated it on the authority of Ibn Ishaq Al-Qushayri. It may be the opposite. Al-Hasan said: His father's name was Azar. Suleiman Al-Taimi said: It is a curse and a shame, and its meaning in their speech is: crooked. Al-Mu'tamir bin Suleiman narrated on the authority of his father, who said: I have heard that it is crooked, and it is the harshest word that Ibrahim said to his father. Al-Dahhak said: The meaning of Azar Al-Sheikh is worry in Persian. Al-Farra' said: It is an attribute of condemnation in their language. It is as if he said, O mistaken one; Whoever raised it? Or as if he said: When Abraham said to his erring father: Who reduced it? And he does not leave because he is doing better. Al-Nahhas said. Al-Jawhari said: Azar is a non-Arab name, and it is derived from Azar so-and-so if he helps him. He supports his people in worshiping idols, and it was said: It is derived from strength, and Al-Azr means strength. On the authority of Ibn Faris. Mujahid Yaman said: Azar is the name of an idol. In this interpretation, it is in the accusative position, meaning: Do you take Azar as a god, do you take idols? It was said: In speech there is an advance and a delay. The estimation: Do you take Azar as idols? I said: So, Azar is a generic name. God knows . Al-Thaalabi said in the Book of Puppetry: The name of my father Ibrahim was what his father Terah gave him, and when he became with Nimrod the custodian of the treasury of his gods, he named him Azar. Mujahid said: Azar is not the name of his father, but rather the name of an idol. He is Abraham, the son of Terah, the son of Nachor, the son of Saru, the son of Argo, the son of Peleg, the son of Eber, the son of Shalakh, the son of Arpakhshad, the son of Shem, the son of Noah, peace be upon him. And Azar has readings: "Azra" with two hamzas, the first open and the second broken; On the authority of Ibn Abbas. On his authority is "Azra" with two open hamzas. It was read in the nominative form, and this was narrated on the authority of Ibn Abbas. The first two readings of it are taken without a hamza. Al-Mahdawi said: Ezra? It was said: It is the name of an idol. It is in the accusative case: "I take ezra," as well as "azra." It is permissible to make azra as derived from the azra, which is the noon, so it is the object of it. It is as if he said: Does power take idols? It is permissible for it to be izr meaning button, the waw was replaced by a hamza. Al-Qushayri said: In protesting against the polytheists, he mentioned the story of Abraham and his response to his father in worshiping idols. The most worthy of people to follow Abraham are the Arabs. They are his descendants. Yes, and remember when Abraham said. Or he was reminded by it that a soul should be vindicated for what it has earned, and it was mentioned when Abraham said. "Azar" was recited, meaning, O Azar, on the singular call, and it is the reading of Abu, Ya'qub, and others. It strengthens the statement of those who say: Azar is the name of my father Ibrahim.

Do you take idols as gods with two objects to take? It is an interrogative that contains the meaning of denial.
Asr al-Tafsir's interpretation of the words of Abu Bakr al-Jaza'iri.

21—Prophet 58

Abu Bakr al-Jazairi (born 1921 AD) (died 2018 AD)

Word Explanation:
Their guidance: that is, their guidance through the need to know their Lord, believe in Him, and obey Him and draw closer to Him.
Statues: Plural of statue, which is an image made in the form of a human being or animal.

To whom you are devoted: that is, you are going to him and following him in worship.
Or are you one of those players: that is, someone who is joking and not serious about what they say or do?

Your Lord is the Lord of the heavens: i.e. the One worthy of worship, the Lord of the heavens and the earth.

Who created them: That is, He created them in creation and creation without any prior example.

I will definitely destroy your idols: that is, I will try to break and destroy your idols.

Chopped: pieces and small pieces.

Except for his greatest idol: Except for his greatest idol, because he didn't break it.

Perhaps they will return to Him: so that they may return to Him and believe in God and be united with Him after the inability of their gods has been revealed.

Meaning of the verse:

Referring to what Almighty God gave to Moses, Aaron and Muhammad, may God's prayers and peace be upon them, by giving them the Torah and the Quran, he mentioned that before that, He was grateful to Abraham, so He gave him Guiding them in their youth, making them aware of Him, His glory, His perfection, and the obligation to believe in Him, the Almighty, and to worship Him alone, and that the worship of anyone other than Him is invalid, said God Almighty. Said: {And We gave Abraham the right guidance before him} And His saying: {And We knew about him} meaning, his suitability for the call and to fulfill it when We taught him {when he said" Meaning At that time when he forbade his father Azar and his people from worshiping anyone other than God, he said, {What are these? Like those to whom you are devoted.} That is, those who are coming near it, following it, and they answered him with what Almighty God told him about them: {They said, "We Found my ancestors worshiping it." Hence they expressed their ignorance, because they did not evidence the validity or benefit of its worship, and they were content with blind imitation, and in this respect their case is the case of all those who worship anyone other than God Almighty. We do, because there is no evidence of it. On the validity of the worshiper's worship other than imitation by someone who saw him worshiping him.

Abraham gave them the same answer that God Almighty had said to him, "He said, 'Indeed, you and your fathers,' i.e. those whose imitations you worshiped as idols, 'had gone astray,' i.e., were away from guidance. .

Taysir al-Karim al-Rahman fi Tafsir Kalam al-Mannan Abd al-Rahman bin Nasir bin al-Saadi (d. 1376 AH)

21:69

And We gave Abraham the right guidance before, and We knew him} until the end of the story, which is what it says: {And We inspired them to do good deeds, and establish prayer, and do good deeds. And they were our worshippers. When God Almighty mentioned Moses and Muhammad, may God bless them and grant them peace, and their two books, He said: Before} i.e.: Before the sending of Moses and Muhammad and the revelation of their books, so God Showed him the kingdom of heaven and earth, and gave him maturity, with which he perfected himself, and called people into it, until no one from the world except Muhammad was given to him, and added maturity to it, because This is maturity according to his situation. And His rank is high, otherwise every believer has maturity according to his faith. {And We were knowledgeable about him} Meaning: We gave him his guidance, and separated for him the message and the character, and chose him in this world and in the hereafter, because We knew that he was worthy of it, and worthy of it , because of his piety and wisdom, and that is why he mentioned his reason with his people, and forbade them from committing shirk, and breaking idols, and bound them to proof, so he said: {When he Said about the father and him, people, what are these idols? (Those whom You have created, and whom You protect with Your hands, as certain beings) to whom You are devoted...

Tafsir Ibn Kathir

Surah: 21. Al-Anbiya -Verse: 69
We said, "O Fire, coolness and peace upon Abraham."

Almighty God said: (O Fire, coolness and peace be upon Abraham.) He said: There was no fire left on earth that was not extinguished.

The Ka'b al-Ahbar said: The fire did not benefit anyone that day, and the fire did not burn Abraham except his chains.

Al-Thawri said, on the authority of al-Amash, on the authority of Shaykh, on the authority of Ali bin Abi Talib: (We said, O Fire, let there be coolness and peace upon Abraham) [He said: It became cool upon him Until he almost died, until it was said: (And peace be upon him)], he said: Do not harm him.

Ibn Abbas and Abu al-Aliyah said: If it had not been true that God Almighty said: (And peace be upon him), then Abraham would have been harmed by its rejection.
Juwaybir said on the authority of al-Dahhak: (Be coolness and peace to Abraham.) He said: They built for him a barn out of spruce firewood, and kindled fire in it all around, so in the morning, nothing would remain of it. It had influence on them until God ended it. He said: He mentioned that Gabriel was with him, wiping the sweat off his face. Apart from this nothing happened to him.

Al-Suddi said: There was a shadow angel with him.

Ibn said...
 confrontation with nimrod

The Quran discusses a very brief conversation between an unrighteous ruler and Abraham. Although the king is not named in the Quran, and this fact is considered the least important in the narrative, outside the Quran, namely in some tafsir, this king has been suggested to be Nimrod. This tafsir by the 14th-century scholar Ibn Kathir contains many embellishments to the story, such as Nimrod claiming divinity for himself. The tafsir describes Nimrod's quarrel with Ibrahim, how he (Nimrod) became extremely angry and became a tyrant in his 'complete disbelief and gross rebellion'.
According to the Romano-Jewish historian Flavius Josephus, Nimrod was a man who set his own will against the will of God. Nimrod declared himself a living god and his subjects worshiped him as such. Nimrod's wife Semiramis was also worshiped as a goddess along with him. (See also Ninus.) Before Abraham's birth, a vision in the stars tells Nimrod and his astrologers of the imminent birth of Abraham, who will put an

end to idolatry. So Nimrod ordered all newborn babies to be killed. However, Abraham's mother runs away into the fields and gives birth to the child in secret. Flavius Josephus mentions that Abraham confronted Nimrod and told him face to face to stop his idolatry, after which Nimrod ordered him to be burned at the stake. Nimrod gathered enough wood from his subjects to burn Abraham in the largest fire the world had ever seen. Yet when the fire is lit and Abraham is thrown into it, Abraham comes out unharmed. There is debate in Islam whether the decision to burn Ibrahim at the crossroads...

Grown up after this incident. Nimrod, who was the king of Babylon, felt that his throne was in danger, and he was losing power because after seeing Abraham coming out safely from the fire, a large part of the society started believing in God and Abraham being God's prophet. Started. By this point, Nimrod was pretending that he was a god himself. Nimrod wanted to debate with him and show his people that he, the king, was indeed God and that Abraham was a liar. Nimrod asked Abraham, "What can your God do that I cannot do?" Ibrahim replied, "My Lord is the One who gives life and death." Nimrod then shouted, "I give life and death! I can bring a man off the street and hang him, and I can pardon a man who was sentenced to death and save his life " Abraham replied, "Okay, my Lord God makes the sun rise from the east. Can you make it rise from the west?" Nimrod became confused. He was defeated in his own game, in his own field and in front of his own people. Abraham...

This event has been considered particularly significant because, from the Muslim perspective, it foreshadowed the prophetic careers of future prophets, most importantly the career of Moses. Abraham's quarrel with the king is interpreted by some as a precursor to Moses' sermon to Pharaoh. Just as the ruler who argued against Abraham claimed divinity for himself, so did the Pharaoh of the Exodus, who refused to listen to the call of Moses and perished in the Red Sea. In this particular incident, scholars have further commented on Abraham's intelligence in employing "rational, intelligent, and goal-oriented" speech, as opposed to nonsensical arguments.

In the eyes of many Muslims, Abraham also symbolizes the highest moral values required of any person. The Quran describes angels coming to Abraham to tell him of the birth of Ismail. It states that, as soon as Abraham saw the messengers, he "hastened to entertain them with a roasted calf. This action is interrupted by...

Lot (Lut)

Lot, also known as Lot in the Old Testament, is a prophet of God in the Quran. According to Islamic tradition, Lot was born in Haran and spent his younger years in Ur, later moving to Canaan with his uncle Abraham. He was sent as a prophet to the cities of Sodom and Gomorrah, and was ordered to preach to their inhabitants on the sinfulness of monotheism and homosexuality and their lustful and violent acts.

Although Lot was not born among the people he was sent to preach, the people of Sodom are regarded as his "brothers" in the Quran. Like the Biblical narrative, the Quran states that Lot's messages were ignored by the cities' residents, and Sodom and Gomorrah were subsequently destroyed. The destruction of cities is traditionally presented as a warning against Islam as well as homosexuality, among other things.

While the Quran does not go into detail about Lot's later life, Islam believes that all prophets were examples of moral and spiritual 'righteousness'. ,

Lot is mentioned a relatively large number of times in the Quran. Many of these fragments place the story of Lot in the line of successive prophets including Noah, Hud, Salih, and Shu'ayb. Islamic scholars have said that these particular prophets represent the initial cycle of prophecy described in the Quran. These narratives generally follow the same pattern: a prophet is sent to a community; The community pays no heed to his warnings, but instead threatens to punish him; God told the Prophet to leave with his followers and the community and its people were subsequently destroyed in punishment. Elsewhere in the Quran, Lot is mentioned along with Ishmael, Elisha, and Jonah as men whom God preferred above the nations.

The Quran states that one day, a group of angels disguised as men came to meet Abraham as guests to inform him of the fact that his wife Sarah was pregnant with Isaac. While there, they also told him that they had been sent by God to Lot's "guilty people" [to destroy them with a "shower of clay stones"] [that Lot and those who believed in him were to be spared, But his wife was to die in the destruction, with the angels saying "she is among those left behind". The Quran also portrays Lot's wife as "an example to the unbelievers" because she was married to a righteous man but refused to believe in his message and was thus condemned to Hell. .

The people of the Twin Cities transgressed God's boundaries. According to the Quran, their sins included inhospitality and robbery, in addition to other abuses and rape. They hated strangers and robbed travelers. It was also their sin of sexual misconduct that was seen as particularly heinous, with Lot rebuking them for going to men with sexual desire rather than women. Lot explained and tried to help them give up their sinful ways, but they ridiculed him and threatened to evict him from the cities. Lot prayed to God and begged to be spared the consequences of his sinful actions.

Then three angels came to Lot as guests in the guise of handsome men. He grieved those people because he felt powerless to protect them from the townspeople. The inhabitants of the city became aware of the visitors and demanded that Lot turn his guests over to them. Distressed and fearful that they would face God's wrath, they suggested legitimate marriage to their daughters as a pious and pure alternative to their unlawful desires, and perhaps as a source of guidance. But they remained adamant and replied, "You surely know we have no need of your daughters. You already know what we want!", referring to their male guests.

The commentators Ibn Kathir, Qurtubi and Tabari do not consider 'daughters' to mean the literal daughters of Lot. They argue that since a prophet is like a father to his nation, Lot was instructing the wicked to turn away from their sins and engage in healthy and holy relationships with the daughters of the nation, i.e. women in general.

Then the angels revealed their true identity to Lot and said to him, "Indeed, We will save you and your family, except your wife; She will be among those left behind" They advised Lot to leave the cities during the night, and told him not to look back. Maintaining his faith in God, Lot left the cities in the darkness of the night, brought with him his followers and believing family members. At last, morning came, and God's command passed, after which the Quran reads, "When Our command came, We overturned the cities and overcame them It rained stones of clay," and thus the fate of the Twin Cities was sealed, bringing destruction and despair and the end of the civilizations of Sodom and Gomorrah.

homosexuality

lgbt in islam

Based on the story of Lot, all schools of Islamic jurisprudence hold that homosexual sex is a sin. Because the Quran states that Lot rebuked his people for having sex with men, in addition to attempting to attack strangers, this incident has traditionally been interpreted as demonstrating Islam's disapproval of both rape and homosexuality. is seen as. Lot's conflict with the people of the Twin Cities is seen as either regarding homosexuality in general or homosexual anal sex specifically. These interpretations have sometimes broadened to condemn homosexuality beyond the physical act, including psychological and social dispositions.

Ishmael (Ishmail)

Ishmael is regarded in Islam as a prophet and messenger and the ancestor of the Ishmaelites. He is the son of Ibrahim, who was born from Hajar. Ismail is also associated with Mecca and the construction of the Kaaba. Ismail is considered the ancestor of Muhammad.

Ishmael is the person known as Ishmael in Judaism and Christianity. These sources include the Quran, Quranic commentaries (tafsir), hadith, historical collections such as those of Muhammad Ibn Jarir al-Tabari, and Isra'iliyya (Islamic texts about Biblical or ancient Israelite figures that originate from Jewish or Christian sources).][2]:13

Birth

Ishmael was the first son of Abraham; His mother was Hajar. There are several versions of the story, some of which include a prophecy about Ishmael's birth. One such example is that of Ibn Kathir (d. 1373), whose account states that an angel told pregnant Hagar to name her child Ishmael and prophesied, "His hand will be over all, and the hand of all Will be against him. His brother." Will rule over all the lands." Ibn Kathir comments that this foretells the leadership of Muhammad.[2]:42

construction of kaaba

At some point, often believed to be after Hagar's death, Ishmael married a woman from the Jurhum tribe, who had settled in the area around Zamzam. Abraham met Ishmael in Mecca and when he reached his house, Ishmael was not there. Instead Ishmael's wife welcomed Abraham, but she was not welcoming or generous towards him. Abraham instructed him to tell Ishmael some version of the statement he was not happy with or to change it.

threshold of her door." When Ishmael returns home and his wife tells him, he learns it is from his father and, taking advice, he divorces the woman. He then marries another woman from Jurhum. Lee. Abraham came once again and met Ishmael's second wife, because Ishmael was away. This wife was very kind and provided food for him. Abraham instructed her to tell Ishmael some version of the statement that he " When Ishmael and his wife arrived, repeating Abraham's statement, Ishmael learned that it was from his father and he took his wife to himself.

There are several versions of the construction of the Kaaba that differ in significant ways, although all have Abraham building or purifying the Kaaba and shortly thereafter, or at some unknown time, God instructed Abraham to establish the Hajj, or pilgrimage. called. These narratives differ as to when these events occurred, whether and how there was supernatural involvement, whether the Black Stone was included or omitted, and whether Ishmael assisted his father. Most of those who say that Ishmael participated in the creation describe that Abraham visited Ishmael for the third time in Mecca,

During which he raised the Kaaba. Some say that Ishmael was looking for a final stone, but Abraham did not accept the one he brought back. Instead an angel brought the black stone, which Abraham set in place. Ishmael was left there to look after the Kaaba and teach others about the Hajj. There are several versions of the origin of the Hajj, and some scholars believe that it reflects Abraham's late association with the Hajj as Islam developed to help remove its connection to early pagan rituals.

Isaac (Ishaq)

The Biblical patriarch Isaac ['Ishaq] is recognized by Muslims as a prophet and messenger of God.] Like Judaism and Christianity, Islam believes that Isaac was the son of the patriarch and prophet Abraham by his wife Sarah. Muslims deeply revere Isaac because they believe that both Isaac and his older half-brother Ishmael continued their father's spiritual legacy through the preaching of God's message after Abraham's death. Isaac is mentioned in fifteen verses of the Quran. Mentioned several times in the Quran, Isaac is considered one of the prophets of Islam.

By the grace of Allah and the covenant with Abraham, Sarah was gifted a child in her old age. Isaac was 10 years old when his half-brother Ishmael left Abraham's house for the wilderness. While living in the desert, Ishmael married a wife named 'Aisha' from one of the daughters of Moab.

in the holy quran

Isaac is mentioned by name fifteen times in the Quran, often along with his father and his son, Jacob (Yakub). The Quran states that Abraham received "the good news of Isaac, the prophet of the righteous", and God blessed them both (37:112). "And We gave him good news about the prophet Isaac, one of the righteous people. And We blessed him and Isaac. And among their descendants there are righteous people and those who clearly do wrong to themselves" in a complete description , when the angels came to Abraham telling him about the future punishment that would be imposed on Sodom and Gomorrah, his wife, Sarah, "laughed, and We told him about Isaac and after (a grandson of) Isaac of Jacob gave good news about" (11: 71-74); And it is further stated that this event will occur despite the old age of Abraham and Sarah. Several verses describe Isaac as a "gift" to Abraham (6:84; 19:49–50), and 29:26–27 states that God "gave prophecy and the Book to his descendants." Made", which has been interpreted to refer to Abraham's two prophet sons, his prophet grandson Jacob, and his prophet great-grandson Joseph. In the Quran, it is later reported that Abraham also praised God for giving him Ishmael and Isaac in old age (XIV:39-41). Elsewhere in the Quran, Isaac is mentioned in the lists: Joseph and his ancestors Abraham. , follows the religion of Isaac and Jacob (12:38) and speaks of God's favor upon them (12:6); All of Jacob's sons testify of their faith and promise to worship the God whom their ancestors, "Abraham, Ishmael and Isaac", worshiped (2:127); And the Quran commands Muslims to believe in the revelations that were given to "Abraham, Ishmael, Isaac, Jacob, and the patriarchs" (2:136; III:84).

Hud

Hud is sometimes identified with Eber, the ancestor of the Ishmaelites and Israelites, mentioned in the Old Testament.

Hud is said to have been the subject of a mulk (Arabic: ملك, kingdom), named after its founder 'Aad, who was a fourth-generation descendant of Noah (his father was Uz, son of Aram, Who were the sons of Shem, who in turn was the son of Noah):

The Ad people, along with their prophet Hud, are mentioned in several places. See especially 26:123-140-Yusuf Ali, and 46:21-26-Yusuf Ali. Their named ancestor 'Aad' was the fourth generation from Noah, who was the son of 'Aus, who was the son of Aram, who was the son of Sam, who was the son of Noah. They occupied a large swath of country in southern Arabia, stretching from Umman at the mouth of the Persian Gulf to Hadramaut and Yemen at the southern end of the Red Sea. They were tall and were great builders. Long, winding paths of sand probably in their dominion (ahqaf) (46:21)

Irrigation was done through canals. They abandoned the true God and oppressed their people. There was a famine of three years on them, but still they did not give any warning. Eventually a terrible blast of wind destroyed them and their land, but a remnant, known as the second 'Ād or Thamud (see below), was saved, and they later suffered the same fate for their sins. had to face. The tomb of the Prophet Hud (Tomb

Nabi Hud) is still traditionally shown at Hadramaut, latitude 16 N and longitude ⁴⁹½ E, about 90 miles north of Mukalla.   There are ruins and inscriptions in the neighbourhood.

—Abdullah Yusuf Ali, The Holy Quran: Text, Translation and Commentary, note 104
 Other tribes claimed to be present in Arabia at this time were the Thamud, Jurhum, Tasam, Jadis, Amim, Midian, Amalek Imlach, Jasim, Qahtan, Banu Yaqtan and others. The Quran cites the location of 'Ad as al-Ḥaqqāf (Arabic: ٱلۡعَحقَاف, "The Sandy Plains", or "The Wind-Curved Sand-Hills"). It is believed to have been in southern Arabia, possibly eastern Yemen and/or western Oman. In November 1991, a settlement was discovered and hypothesized to be salvaged, which is mentioned in the Quran as Iram Dhat al-Imad ("Iram of the Pillars" or "Iram of the Tentpoles"), and probably Must have been the capital of ʿĀd. However, archaeologist Juris Zarin, one of the members of the original expedition, later concluded that the discovery did not represent a city called Ubar. In a 1996 interview on this subject, he said:

If you look at classical texts and Arab historical sources, Ubar refers to a region and group of people, not a specific city. People always ignore it. This is very clear on Ptolemy's 2nd century map of the area. It says "Iobarite" in big letters. And in his text that comes with the maps, he is very clear about it. It was only the final medieval version of the One Thousand and One Nights, in the fourteenth or fifteenth century, that romanticized Ubar and turned it into a city rather than a region or people.

The Moroccan mystic Abdulaziz ad-Dabbagh gives detailed information about the hood: according to him, 53:50
This points to the fact that Hud was sent to the second 'Tribe of Ad', who lived after Noah. Earlier the tribe of 'Ad had a messenger named Huwaid, whose message was to be revived by Hud, and the tribe was destroyed by God with stones and fire. Hood was the son of Ebar (see Ebar for his genealogy in Islam) and Iram was the name of one of the tribes of 'Aad, specifically sent to Hood (see Iram in the Quran).

Miracle

According to a tafsir in Ibn Qayyim al-Jawziyya's analysis book, Madarij Saliken, which is cited by Ibn Abi al-Izz in his sirah (commentary) of al-Aqida al-Tahawiyya, the Hud has a miracle, which is This is indicated by verses 56-58:

(56) "We can only say that some of our gods have become a bad influence on you." He replied: "I call God to witness, and you also be witness, that I am clear from whomever you involve (in your affairs)... except him. Conspiracy against me as much as you want. Create, and don't give me any respite
(57) I believe in God who is my Lord and your Lord. There is no creature roaming on the earth which has not held firmly with its forelimbs. Surely the path of my Lord is straight.

(58) If you turn away, then (remember) I have already delivered to you the message with which I was sent. My Lord will raise up others in your place, and you will not be able to prevail over him. Surely my Lord watches over everything."

—Quran, Surah 11 (Hud), verses 56-58
Both Ibn Qayyim and Ibn Abi al-Izz examine this series of verses as the incident when Hud fought alone against the entire nation of 'Aad, the entire city harming him psychologically and physically. was defeated only by the miraculous power shown by Had, which was the result of his strong belief in protection from God. Omar Sulayman al-Ashkar, a Salafi scholar of tafsir, cited this literature in his book, while his brother, Muhammad Sulaiman al-Ashkar, a professor at the Islamic University of Medina, also supported this narrative about the miracle of Hud. His own tafsir, Zubdat in Tafsir min Fatah al-Qadir, by Firanda Andirja, lecturer at Al-Masjid al-Haram, sheds further light on this miracle. According to a tafsir of the entire Surah Hud by scholars, 'Ad was a powerful empire that existed before the era of Abraham and Nimrod, and they were tyrannical towards other civilizations at that time.

Tafsir Ibn Kathir

Surah: 11. Hud -Verse: 50

And to Aad, to his brother Hud, he said, "O my people, worship God. You have no gods except Him. You are nothing but inventors."

God Almighty says, "And We sent their brother Hud to Ad, and ordered them to worship God alone without any partners, and forbade them from the idols they had made and the names of gods they invented. Was.

Jacob (Yakub)

Ya'qub ibn Ishaq ibn Ibrahim (Jacob, son of Isaac, son of Abraham), later renamed Israel.

Recognized by Muslims as an Islamic prophet.

He is said to have preached monotheism like his ancestors: Abraham, Ishmael and Isaac.

Jacob is mentioned sixteen times in the Quran. Two further references to "Israel" are believed to mention Jacob. In most of these references, Jacob, identified as the son of Isaac, is mentioned as an ancient and pious prophet along with fellow Hebrews, who lived in "the company of the chosen" and the unity of Allah throughout time. Emphasized on. his life. In Islam, like Judaism and Christianity, it is stated that Jacob had twelve sons, who went on to become the fathers of the twelve tribes of Israel. Jacob plays an important role in the story of his son Joseph. The Quran further makes it clear that Allah made a covenant with Jacob, and Jacob was made a faithful leader by divine command. His grandfather Abraham, his father Isaac, his uncle Ishmael, and his son Joseph are all recognized as Islamic prophets.

Jacob's name appears sixteen times in the Quran. Although many of these verses praise him rather than describe an example of his legend, the Quran nevertheless records many important events from his life. Muslim tradition and literature The earliest event related to Jacob in the Quran is that of angels (malaikah) giving the "good news" to Abraham and Sarah about the future birth of a prophetic son by the name of Isaac and also a prophet. Grandson by the name of Jacob. The Quran says:

When he turned away from them and those they worshiped besides God, We provided him Isaac and Jacob, and We made each of them a prophet.

—Quran, Sura 19 (Maryam), verse 49[

The Quran also mentions that Abraham taught the faith of pure monotheism to his sons, Ishmael and Isaac, as well as Jacob. The Quran records Abraham saying to Ishmael, Isaac and Jacob: "O my sons! God has chosen the faith for you; so do not die except in the faith of Islam." The Quran also mentions gifts given to Jacob. Such is the strength of his faith, which grew stronger as he grew up. The Quran mentions that Jacob was "guided"; They were given "knowledge"; was "inspired"; And they were given "the tongue of truth to hear." The Quran later states the following regarding Jacob:
The Quran later states the following regarding Jacob:

And We provided him with Isaac and a grandson, Jacob, as a further gift, and We made each of them a righteous man.

And We made them leaders, guides (men) by Our command, and We sent them inspiration and they served Us (and only Us) continuously.

—Quran, Surah 21 (Al-Anbiya), verses 72-73

And remember our servants Abraham, Isaac and Jacob, who were masters of power and vision.

Verily We chose them for a special (purpose) – to announce the message of the Last Day.

They, in our view, truly belonged to the company of the chosen and the good.

—Quran, Sura 38 ('The Sorrowful'), verses 45-47

Moses (Musa)

Prophet and Savior of Israel

During the time of Joseph and Jacob the Israelites settled in the land of Goshen, but a new Pharaoh arose who oppressed the children of Israel. At this time Moses was born to his father Amram, who was the son (or descendant) of Kohath the Levite, who came to Egypt with the house of Jacob; His mother was Jochebed (also Yocheved), a relative of Kohath. Moses had an older (seven years older) sister, Miriam, and an older (three years older) brother, Aaron. Pharaoh had ordered that all male Hebrew children born be drowned in the Nile River, but Moses' mother placed him in an ark and hid the ark in the bushes along the river bank, where the child was discovered and Pharaoh's daughter adopted him, and raised him as an Egyptian. One day, after Moses became an adult, he killed an Egyptian who was beating a Hebrew.

Moses, to escape Pharaoh's execution, fled to Midian (a desert country south of Judah), where he married Zipporah.

There, at Mount Horeb, God appeared to Moses in the form of a burning bush, revealing to Moses his name YHWH (probably pronounced Jehovah). Promised Land (Canaan). During the journey, God tried to kill Moses, but Zipporah saved his life. Moses returned to carry out God's command, but God overruled Pharaoh, and only after God subjected Egypt to ten plagues did Pharaoh relent. Moses led the Israelites to the border of Egypt, but their God hardened Pharaoh's heart once again, so that he destroyed Pharaoh and his army at the crossing of the Red Sea as a sign of His power to Israel and the nations. Could.

After defeating the Amalekites at Rephidim, Moses led the Israelites to Mount Sinai, where he was given the Ten Commandments from God, written on stone tablets. However, because Moses remained on the mountain for a long time, some people feared that he might have died, so they made an idol of a golden calf and worshiped it, thus disobeying God and Moses and angering them. Moses, in anger, broke the tablets and later ordered the extermination of those who worshiped the golden idol, which was melted down and fed to the idolaters. He also wrote the Ten Commandments on a new set of tablets. Later at Mount Sinai, Moses and the elders entered into a covenant by which Israel would become YHWH's people, obey His laws, and YHWH would be their God. Moses gave God's laws to Israel, established a priesthood under the sons of Moses' brother Aaron, and destroyed those Israelites who turned away from his worship.

In his final act at Sinai, God gives Moses instructions for the Tabernacle, the mobile temple through which he will travel with Israel to the Promised Land.

From Sinai, Moses led the Israelites to the Paran Desert on the border of Canaan. From there he sent twelve spies into the country. The spies returned with samples of the land's fertility but warned that its inhabitants were demons. The people were afraid and wanted to return to Egypt, and some rebelled against Moses and God. Moses told the Israelites that they were not worthy to inherit the land, and would wander in the wilderness for forty years until the generation that had refused to enter Canaan died, so that their children could inherit the land. Be done. Later, Korah is punished for leading a rebellion against Moses.

When forty years had passed, Moses led the Israelites east across the Dead Sea to the areas of Edom and Moab. There they escaped the temptation of idolatry, conquered the lands of Og and Sihon in Transjordan, received God's blessing through the prophet Balaam, and massacred the Midianites, who by the end of the Exodus journey had become... .
On the banks of the Jordan River, within sight of the land, Moses gathered the tribes. After recounting their wanderings, they told God's laws according to which they should live on the land, sang songs of praise and blessed the people, and gave Joshua their authority under which they would own the land. Moses then climbed Mount Nebo, looked at the Promised Land spread out before him, and died at the age of one hundred and twenty.

lawgiver of israel
Moses is revered among Jews today as "Israel's lawgiver", and he provides several sets of laws over the course of four books. The first is the Covenant Code, the terms of the covenant that God gave to the Israelites at Mount Sinai. Embodied in the covenant are the Decalogue (Ten Commandments, Exodus 20:1–17), and the Book of the Covenant (Exodus 20:22–23:19). The entire book of Leviticus constitutes a second body of law, the book of Numbers begins another set, and the book of Deuteronomy begins yet another set.

Moses is traditionally considered the author of the four books and the Book of Genesis that comprise the Torah, the first section of the Hebrew Bible.

historical

Scholars hold varying opinions on the position of Moses in scholarship. For example, William G. According to Dever, the consensus of modern scholars is that the biblical figure of Moses is largely mythological, while it is also believed that "a Moses-like figure may have existed somewhere in southern Transjordan in the mid-13th century BC." " and that "archeology can do nothing to prove or confirm anything one way or the other". However, according to Solomon Negosian, there are actually three prevailing views among Biblical scholars: one is that Moses is not a historical person. The second approach attempts to establish the decisive role they played in Israelite religion, and the third argues that there are elements of both history and legend that show "these issues are hotly debated among scholars. There are unresolved issues".

According to Brian Britt, there is disagreement among scholars when discussing matters related to Moses that threatens impasse.[According to the official Torah commentary for Orthodox Judaism, if the historical Moses existed, he would be described as "folklorist, It is irrelevant to call him a "national hero".[

Jan Assmann argues that it cannot be known whether Moses ever lived because there is no trace of him outside tradition. Although the names of Moses and other people in the Biblical stories are Egyptian and contain actual Egyptian elements, no extra-Biblical source points explicitly to Moses. There are no references to Moses in any Egyptian sources before the 4th century BC, long after he is believed to have lived. No contemporary Egyptian sources mention Moses or the events of Exodus–Deuteronomy, nor has any archaeological evidence been discovered in Egypt or the Sinai Wilderness to support a story in which he is the central figure. David Adams Leeming states that Moses is a mythological hero and central figure in Hebrew mythology. The Oxford Companion to the Bible states that the historicity of Moses is the most reasonable (though not unbiased) assumption to be made about him because his absence would leave a void that cannot be explained.

The Oxford Bible Study states that although some modern scholars are inclined to support the traditional view that Moses himself wrote the five books of the Torah, there are certainly those who view Moses' leadership as being so firmly based in Israel's corporate memory. Believe that it cannot be dismissed as sacred.

The story of Moses' discovery follows the familiar motif in ancient Near Eastern mythology of the ruler who arose from humble origins. For example, in Sargon of Akkad's account of the Genesis (23rd century BC):

My mother, the high priestess, became pregnant; secretly he bored me

 He put me in a basket of rushes, he sealed my lid with bitumen
He threw me into the river which was flowing over me.
The story of Moses, like that of the other patriarchs, probably had a substantial oral prehistory (he is mentioned in the Book of Jeremiah and the Book of Isaiah) and his name is apparently very ancient, as the tradition found in Exodus no longer retains its original meaning. Doesn't understand. Yet, the completion of the Torah and its

elevation to the center of post-exilic Judaism was also about combining older texts as well as writing new ones –

The final Pentateuch was based on existing traditions. Isaiah, written during the exile (i.e., the first half of the 6th century BCE), testifies to the tension between the people of Judah and the Jews returning after the exile ("Golah"), stating that God He is the father of Israel and the history of Israel begins with the Exodus, not with Abraham. From this and similar evidence (e.g., the Book of Ezra and the Book of Nehemiah) it can be concluded that the image of Moses and the story of the Exodus must have been prominent among the people of Judah during the time of the exile. and thereafter, served to oppose returning exiles to support their claims to the land.

A theory developed by Cornelis Teale in 1872, which has proven influential, argued that Jehovah was a Midianite deity, introduced to the Israelites by Moses, whose father-in-law Jethro was a Midianite priest. It was to such Moses that Jehovah revealed his true name, which was hidden from the patriarchs who knew him only as El Shaddai. Against this view is the modern consensus that most Israelites were natives of Palestine. Martin Knoth argued that the Pentateuch uses the figure of Moses, originally linked to the legends of the Transjordan conquest, as a narrative to tie together four of the five, originally independent, themes of that work. As a bracket or late response device. Manfred Görg [de] and Rolf Kraus [de], the latter somewhat sensationally, have suggested that the story of Moses is a distortion or adaptation of the historical Pharaoh Amenemose (circa 1200 BC). ,

Who was dismissed from office and whose name was later simplified to msy (Mose). Aidan Dodson considers this hypothesis "interesting, but beyond proof". Rudolf Smend argues that the two details about Moses that were most likely to be historical are his name, of Egyptian origin, and his marriage to a Midianite woman, details which are unlikely to have been invented by the Israelites; In Smend's view, all other details given in the Biblical narrative are so legendary that they cannot be seen as accurate data. The name of Mesha, king of Moab, has been linked to Moses. Mesha is also associated with stories of the Exodus and conquest, and the stories about him share many motifs with the Exodus story and Israel's war with Moab (2 Kings 3). Moab rebels against oppression, leads his people out of Israel, just as Moses does from Egypt, and his first-born son is killed at the wall of Kir-hareseth, as in the story of Exodus. The slaughter of Israel's firstborn was condemned in 145 BC, with Calvinist theologian Peter Leithart describing it as "a demonic Passover that spares Mesha while wrath burns against his enemies

An Egyptian version of the story, which resembles the story of Moses, is found in Manetho, who, according to the summary in Josephus, wrote that a certain Osarseph, a Heliopolitan priest, became overseer of a group of lepers when Amenophis, following his promptings, had Amenhotep, son of Hapu, cast out all the lepers of Egypt in order to purify the land so that it could see the gods. The lepers are gathered at Avaris, the former capital of the Hyksos, where Osaresef prescribes for them all that is prohibited in Egypt, while banning all that is permitted in Egypt. They invited the Hyksos to invade Egypt again, rule with them for 13 years – Ossarsef then assumed the name Moses – and then were driven out.

Other Egyptian figures who have been presented as candidates for a Moses-like historical figure include Prince Ahmose-Ankh and Ramose, who was a son of Pharaoh Ahmose I, or a man associated with the family of Pharaoh Thutmose III. Israel Nohal proposes to identify Moses with Irsu, a Shasu who, according to Papyrus Harris I and the Elephantine Stele, took power in Egypt with the support of the "Asiatics" (people of the Levant) after the death of Queen Tusret. Was; After coming to power, Irsu and his supporters disrupted Egyptian rituals, "treated the gods like people" and stopped offering offerings to the Egyptian gods. Eventually the new pharaoh Setankhte defeated and expelled them, and while fleeing they left behind large quantities of gold and silver which they had stolen from the temples.

Aaron (Harun)

In Islam, Harun ibn Imran is a prophet and messenger of God, and the elder brother of the Prophet Musa (Moses). He preached to the Israelites in the Exodus with his brother (Moses). Need clarification

There are many references to Aaron in the Quran, both named and unnamed. It states that he was a descendant of Ibrahim (Abraham) [verification failed] and makes it clear that both he and Moses were sent together to warn Pharaoh about God's punishment. It further states that Moses had previously prayed to God to strengthen his own ministry with Aaron[clarification needed] and that Aaron helped Moses because he was also a prophet, and had a good knowledge of speech and discourse. Was very eloquent in matters. The Quran states that both Moses and Aaron were tasked with establishing dwellings for the Israelites in Egypt and transforming those dwellings into places of worship for God.

As described in the Quran, the incident of the golden calf portrays Aaron in a positive light. The Quran states that Aaron was entrusted with the leadership of Israel while Moses was at Ṭūr Sīnāʾ (Mount Sinai) for a period of forty days. It says that Aaron tried his best to stop the worship of the golden calf, which was not built by Aaron but by an evil man named Samiri. [verification failed] Quran 20:85-95 When Moses returned from Mount Sinai, he rebuked Aaron for allowing the worship of the idol, upon which Aaron begged Moses not to blame him when he had a hand in its construction. There was no role. [verification failed] The Quran then states that Moses lamented here the sins of Israel, and said that only he had authority over himself and Aaron.

Aaron is later commemorated in the Quran as someone who had "clear authority" and who was "guided on the right path". It further states that the memory of Aaron was left to the people who came after him and that he has been blessed by God along with his brother. The Quran also says that the people 'Mary (Arabic: مريم, Mary) the mother of Jesus. Was called 'Ko'. Muslim scholars debated who exactly this "Harun" was in reference to his historical personality, with some saying it was a reference to the Aaron of the Exodus, and that the word "sister" was merely a metaphor. represents or spiritual connection between the two figures, made more clear when Mary was a descendant of the priestly line of Aaron,
While others considered it to be another righteous man living at the time of Jesus Christ by the name of "Aaron". Most scholars agree with the former perspective, and spiritually associate Mary with Aaron's actual sister, her namesake Miriam (Arabic: مريم, Hebrew: מִרְיָם), whom she resembled in many ways. The Quran also states that, centuries later, when the coffin (Arabic: تابوت, Ark of the Covenant) was returned to Israel, it contained "the remains of the family of Moses and the remains of the family of Aaron".

Joseph (Yusuf)

Yusuf Ibn Yaqub Ibn Ishaq Ibn Ibrahim, romanized: Yusuf Ibn Yaqub Ibn Ishaq Ibn Ibrahim, literally 'Joseph, son of Jacob, son of Isaac, son of Abraham') is a prophet mentioned in the Quran. and corresponds to Joseph, a figure from the Hebrew and Christian Bibles who is said to have lived in Egypt before the New Kingdom. Of Jacob's children, Joseph reportedly had the gift of prophecy. Although the stories of other prophets are presented in many surahs, the complete story of Joseph appears in only one: Yusuf. It is said to be the most detailed narrative of the Quran, containing more details than its Biblical counterpart.

Yusuf is believed to have been the eleventh son of Yakub (Arabic: يعقوب) and, according to many scholars, his favorite. Ibn Kathir wrote, "Jacob had twelve sons who were the ancestors of the tribes of the Israelites. The noblest of them, the noblest, the noblest, was Joseph." The story begins with Joseph telling his father a dream, which Jacob recognizes. In addition to the role of God in their lives, the story of Joseph and Zulaikha (Potiphar's wife in the Old Testament) became a popular subject of Persian literature and was expanded upon over the centuries.

The story of Joseph in the Quran is a continuous narrative. It contains over one hundred verses, covering several years; They "present a wonderful variety of science and characters in a tight plot, and offer a dramatic portrayal of some of the fundamental themes of the Quran." The Quran notes the importance of the story in the third verse: "And We narrate to you Asanal-Qaish (literally 'the best (or most beautiful) stories')." Most scholars believe this refers to the story of Joseph; Others, including al-Tabari, believe that it refers to the Quran as a whole. It documents the execution of God's decisions despite the challenge of human intervention ("And God has complete power and control over His affairs; but the majority of mankind do not know it").

before the dream

Muhammad at-Sabari provides detailed commentary on the narrative in his chapter on Joseph, citing the opinions of other renowned scholars. In al-Sabri's chapter, the physical beauty of Joseph and his mother Rahil is introduced; He was said to have "more beauty than any other human being." [His father, Jacob, gave him up to his eldest sister to be raised. Al-Abari writes that there was no greater love than that which Joseph's aunt felt for him, for she raised him as her own child; She was reluctant to return it to Jacob, so she kept it with her until her death. According to al-Abari, she could do this because of a belt given to her by her father, Isaac: "If someone else acquired it by deceit from the person who was supposed to have it, he would be completely Will be subject to the will." Of the original owner."
Joseph's aunt puts the belt on Joseph when Jacob is absent; She accuses Joseph of stealing it, and he remains with her until her death. Jacob is reluctant to leave Joseph, and supports him when they are together.

The narrative begins with a dream, and ends with its interpretation. As the sun appeared on the horizon, bathing the earth in morning glory, Joseph (Jacob's son) woke up happy from a pleasant dream. Filled with excitement, he runs to his father and tells him what he saw.

Joseph said to his father: "O my father! I saw eleven stars and the sun and the moon: I saw them bowing before me!

—Quran 12:4[12]

According to Ibn Kathir, Jacob knows that Joseph will become important in this world and the next. He believes that the stars represent his brothers; The sun and moon represent him and Joseph's mother, Rachel. Jacob tells Joseph to keep the dream a secret to protect him from the jealousy of his brothers, who are unhappy with Jacob's love for Joseph.

He prophesies that Joseph will be the one through whom the prophecy of his grandfather Abraham will be fulfilled: his progeny will keep the light of Abraham's house alive and spread God's message to mankind. Abu Ya'ala interprets Jacob's response as an understanding that the inclination of the planets, the Sun, and the Moon toward Joseph represents "something scattered that God has united." They are plotting against you: for Satan is the avowed enemy of humanity. Thus your Lord has chosen you and given you the knowledge of the interpretation of dreams, and has completed His blessing upon you and upon the family of Jacob as He had completed it. Your first ancestors: Ibrahim and Is-Haq (Isaac). Your Lord is Knowing, Wise" (Quran, Surah 12 (Yusuf) verses 5-6).

Joseph does not tell his brothers about his dream (contrary to the Hebrew Bible version), but they remain very jealous. Al-Abari writes

They said to each other, "Verily Joseph and his brother (Benjamin) are dearer to our father than us, even though we are an army ('USBH). By USBH they meant a group, for they were ten in number . They said, "Our father is clearly in a deranged state." Joseph has a mild disposition and is respectful, kind, and considerate, like his brother Benjamin; both are sons of Rachel. From a hadith (Arabic: حديث, literally 'statement'):

Narrated Abu Huraira: Some people asked the Prophet: "Who is the most honorable among the people?" He replied, "The most honorable among them is the one who is most God-fearing." They said, "O Prophet of God! We do not ask about this." He said,

"Then the most honorable person is Joseph, Nabiyullah, literally 'Prophet of God'), son of Nabiyyah, son of Khalilillah, literally 'Friend of God.')."

—Sahih al-Bukhari, collected by Muhammad al-Bukhari[

death and burial

According to Islamic tradition, the Biblical Joseph is buried next to the Cave of the Patriarchs in Hebron, where a medieval structure known as the Castle of Joseph (Arabic: Yusuf-Kalah) is located.

The story of Joseph provides an understanding of Quranic models of sexuality and gender and hegemonic masculinity. A prophet very different from other prophets in the Quran is encountered in the surah, but all prophets are chosen to guide other human beings to God. Joseph is similar to the other prophets because his story conveys God's message, and his story "begins and ends with God. This is why all prophets are similar: their sole purpose is to highlight God's divinity, but the other prophets They have no significance in comparison to. "

Ibn Kathir used Joseph's resistance to Zulaikha as the basis for saying that humans are saved by God because they fear him. Feminist scholars such as Barbara Freire Stovaiser consider this interpretation derogatory to women, suggesting that women do not have the same relationship: "In both hadiths the concept of fitnah (social chaos, social anarchy, temptation) appears as a symbol of which indicate that to be female is to be sexually aggressive and, therefore, dangerous to social stability. The Quran, however, reminds humans to focus on submission to God. However, attraction and love, Related factors make their love affair impossible.

Tafsir ahsanul bayan

Sura Yusuf 12:10

One of them said, "Do not kill Joseph, but cast him into a blind well so that (1) an (oncoming) caravan may pick him up. If you must do so, then do this (2)."

10.1 When a well is called and the Ghaybah mentions its bottom and depth, the well is still deep and no one sees what has fallen into it. When he even mentioned the depth of the well, he started exaggerating.

10.2 That is, when newly arrived travelers come near a well in search of water, it is possible that someone may discover that a person has fallen into the well and they may take him out and take him with them. This proposal was presented by a brother of Azra Shafqat. Compared to murder, this proposal is indeed sympathetic. The jealousy of the brothers became so fierce that they too timidly proposed that if something had to be done, then do it like this.

Tafsir Jalalain

12:24

And she certainly wanted him, she wanted to have sexual intercourse with him, and he wanted her too, he too wanted the same, if it had not been that he had not seen the proof of his Lord: Ibn 'Abbas said, ' Jacob called him to appear before him, and he struck his [Joseph's] breast, after which his [sexual] desire was driven away [from his body] by means of his nails (Response of the Law,' If it had not been', omitted: [understood to be] la-jama'ah, 'he would have slept with her'). So it was, that We showed him the proof, so that We could drive away from him [the actions of] evil, treachery and wickedness. Verily he was among Our devoted servants in terms of obedience (mukhalasana: a different text has mukhalasana, in other words, 'chosen/pure [servants]').

Tafseer As Saadi

12:50

When the messenger returned to the king and the people and told them about the interpretation of Yusuf (peace be upon him), they were astonished to hear the interpretation and were extremely happy. He said, "Bring him to me." Take Joseph out of prison and present him before me. Therefore, when the king's messenger came to Yusuf (peace and blessings of Allaah be upon him) and asked him to appear before the king, he refused to come out of prison until his crime was completely revealed to the people. . This shows his patience, intelligence and intelligence. At that time, he said to the king's messenger: "Go back to the king." He was bitten. Because their matter is completely clear and obvious ("My Lord knows their deceit, all know. "

Tafsir ahsanul bayan

12:100

And he made his parents (2) sit on his throne and they all fell down in prostration before him (2) Then he said, Father! This is the interpretation of my first dream (3) My Lord made it come true, He did me a great favor when He brought me out of prison (4) and brought you out of this desert of disagreement (5). Satan has put into me and my brothers (6) My Lord is the best planner of what He wills and He is very knowledgeable and wise.

100.1 Some commentators believe that this was the stepmother and great aunt because Joseph's real mother died after Benjamin was born. Hazrat Yaqoob (s.a.) married his wife after his death and this aunt went to Egypt with Hazrat Yaqoob (s.a.) (Fath al-Qadir), but Imam Ibn Tabari has said on the contrary that Yusuf (Peace be upon him) His mother was not dead and she was his real mother. (Ibn Kathir)

100.2 Some have translated this as bowing before Yusuf (peace be upon him) in humility and respect. But the words of (12 (وَكَرُّوْ لَهِ سوجَّدَ. Yusuf: 100) show that they prostrated Yusuf (peace be upon him) on the ground, that is, the meaning of this sajdah is prostration. However, this sajdah is a respectful sajdah, sajdah is not an act of worship, and sajdah is acceptable in the Shari'a of Hazrat Yakub (peace be upon him). In Islam, Sajda Tajimi has also been prohibited for the prohibition of Shirk and now Sajda Tajimi is also not permissible for anyone.

100.3 That is, what Hazrat Yusuf (a.s.) saw in his dream, after going through so many trials, its interpretation finally came out that Allah Ta'ala placed Hazrat Yusuf (a.s.) on the throne and his parents along with him All the brothers bowed their heads to him.

100.4 The blessings of Allah did not mention getting out of the well so that the brothers would not be embarrassed. This is prophetic morality.

5.100 Canaan was a desert compared to a civilized area like Egypt, so it was called Bedouin.

100.6 It is also an example of good manners that the brothers were not blamed and that the devil was the cause of this act.

Job (Ayyub)

Job is known as a prophet in Islam and is mentioned in the Quran. The story of Job in Islam parallels the story of the Hebrew Bible, although the main emphasis is on Job's steadfast devotion to God; There is no mention of Job's discussion with friends in the Quranic text, but later Muslim literature states that Job had brothers who argued with the man about the cause of his trouble. Some Muslim commentators also considered Ayyub to be the ancestor of the Romans. Islamic literature also comments on the time and place of Job's prophetic ministry, saying that he came after Joseph in the prophetic chain and preached to his own people rather than being sent to any specified community. The tradition further states that Job will be in heaven "the leader of the group of those who endured patiently".

Tafsir

Ibn Kathir narrates the story as follows. Job was a very rich man who had a lot of land, many animals and children – all of which were lost and soon he suffered from skin disease as a test from God. He was suffering from wounds in which insects were crawling. He remained steadfast and patient, so God eventually delivered him from the disease.

The dynasty of Ayyubid was an important area of study for many early Islamic scholars. A popular belief among early commentators was that Job came from the lineage of Esau, son of Isaac. Although different commentators give different genealogies related to Job, they all trace his lineage back to Abraham through Isaac's son Esau. Scholars who linked Job's genealogy to Abraham used the following Quranic verse as the basis for their view:

"This was the argument about Us which We gave Abraham (to use) against his people. We increase in degree whomever We wish, for your Lord is full of wisdom and knowledge. We gave him (Abraham) Isaac and Jacob, all provided (three) We guided; and before him We guided Noah and his descendants David, Solomon, Job, Joseph, Moses and Aaron. Thus do We reward the righteous. "

Muslim historical literature highlights the story of Job and describes him as a late descendant of the patriarch Noah. Similar to the Hebrew Bible narrative, Ibn Kathir mentions that Satan heard God's angels talking about Job as the most faithful man of his generation. Job, being God's chosen prophet, was devoted to daily prayer and often cried out to God, thanking God for blessing him with abundant wealth and a large family. But Satan planned to turn the God-fearing Job away from God and wanted Job to fall into unbelief and corruption. Therefore, God allowed Satan to afflict Job with distress and intense illness and pain, because God knew that Job would never turn away from his Lord. Although Job's

Even though his property was destroyed and he faced many calamities, he remained steadfast in his worship of God and committed to his religion. Satan then appears to Job in the guise of an old man and suggests that God is not rewarding Job for his prayers. However, Job rebuked Satan and told him that God is omniscient and does what suits him best. It is said that Satan then, having failed to tempt Job, turned to Job's wife, who was also a faithful woman. Satan reminded Job's wife of her life before Job's suffering and how they were abundant in family and fortune. Job's wife, although she did not lose faith, began to cry bitterly and prayed to Job to ask God to remove this affliction from the house. Job, in his grief, scolded his wife and told her that this suffering would be relatively short-lived and without thinking he told her that he would hit her with 100 blows.

Or complaining. After Job recovered, God ordered him to take some grass and strike it 100 times. By doing this, Job fulfilled his promise to God but did not hurt Him. This Islamic narrative has now become symbolic and is often used by Islamic preachers as a reminder to be kind to wives.

Philip K. Hittite claimed that the subject was Arabia and the setting was Northern Arabia.

Jonah (Yunus)

Yunus ibn Matta is a prophet and messenger of God (Allah). Yunus is traditionally considered highly important in Islam as a prophet who was loyal to God and delivered his messages. Yunus is the only prophet of the Twelve Minor Prophets of the Bible whose name is given in the Quran. The tenth chapter of the Quran is named after him.

In the Quran, Yunus is mentioned several times by name, as the Messenger of Allah, and as Dhul-Nun.

The ninth-century Persian historian al-Tabari wrote that, while Jonah was inside the fish, "none of his bones or members was injured". Al-Tabari also wrote that Allah made the fish's body transparent, allowing Yunus to see "the wonders of the depth" [and Yunus heard all the fish praising Allah. The tenth-century poet Kisai Marwazi recorded that Yunus's father was seventy years old when he was born[and that he died soon after,[leaving Yunus's mother with nothing but a wooden spoon, Which became later. Become a cornucopia.

Tafsir Ibne Kasir

37:142
Then a (big) fish swallowed him because he had done something worthy of blame.

Then Allah ordered a large fish from the Green Sea (i.e. the Mediterranean Sea) to come tearing the sea and swallow Yunus, peace be upon him, without biting his flesh or breaking his bones. The fish came and Yunus, peace be upon him, fell into the water, and the fish swallowed him and carried him away, and traveled with him across all the seas. When Yunus remained in the stomach of the fish for some time, he thought that he was dead; Then he moved his head, legs, arms, and saw that he was alive. He prayed in the belly of the fish, and one of the things he said in his main prayer was:

"O Lord, I have created a place for your worship where no other person could reach."

There was disagreement among them as to how much time he spent in the fish's belly.

Some said three days; This was the view from Qatada.
 Some said seven days; This was the idea of Ja'far as-Sadiq, may Allah be pleased with him.

Some said forty days; This was Abu Malik's idea.

Mujahid narrates from ash-Shaabi, "He swallowed it in the morning and threw it out in the evening."

And only Allah knows best how much time it actually was.

Allah says,
Asr al-Tafsir's interpretation of the words of Abu Bakr al-Jazairi

68 pen 48
Abu Bakr al-Jazairi (born 1921 AD) (died 2018 AD)

Word Explanation:

Leave me and the liars: that is, leave me and the liars, that is, do not believe.

With this Hadith: i.e. with the Holy Quran.

We will tempt them: that is, we will bring them down, step by step, until we put them in torment.

And I command them: that is, I allow them.

My story is strong: that is, serious, strong and unbearable.

They are burdened with debt: that is, they are burdened with what they give you, that is, they are burdened with a heavy burden.

Or do they have an invisible, i.e. protected, tablet?

They write: That is, they transmit what they claim and say.

And don't be like the whale's owner: i.e. eunuchs, boredom and haste.

He is sad: that is, full of sorrow.

In the open: i.e. empty land.

He is reprehensible: but when he repented, he was rejected, although he was not reprehensible.

Therefore his Lord chose him: that is, chose him.

They will make you tremble with your eyes: that is, they will look at you with such intensity that you will almost faint.

He is only a man: that is, Muhammad, may God bless him and grant him peace.

To the world: that is, to humans and jinns, so he is not mad, as the invalids say.
Meaning of the verse:
After the severe rebuke of the lying polytheists, which had no effect on their souls at all, God Almighty said to His Messenger {So leave me} i.e., on the basis of that, leave me and whoever on this Hadith Does not believe, i.e. leave me and them. The meaning of the Hadith is Noble Quran: {We will bring them back} which means, We will bring them down degree by degree {from where they do not know. Until they perish in the suffering resulting from their denial and shirk. And Almighty God says: {And I will give them hope that indeed My plan is firm} That is, I will give them respite, so I will not hasten their punishment, so I will extend their livelihood and make them healthy in body As long as they see that we have respect for them and that they are better than the believers, then we will take them. This is My grave and unbearable conspiracy, and Almighty God says: "Or do you ask for a reward from them, so that they are burdened with debt?" Meaning, rather, do you demand a reward from them in exchange for conveying this, so they are burdened with debt,
Meaning, rather, do you demand a reward from them in exchange for delivering the message? This, so they are burdened with debt, that is, they feel a heavy burden for the reward they give you, so they owe you Do not believe and do not follow you. At your invitation. Or do they have a preserved tablet, then they write down what it says and confirm it, and the answer is no. Then O our Messenger, be patient with them in you and in the judgment of your Lord, and follow your call, and do not be distracted by their disbelief or stubbornness, and do not be like Yunus bin Matka, the companion of the whale, i.e. boredom and In lack of patience. When he called out in sorrow, that is, filled with sorrow, he said, "There is no one worthy of worship except You, glory be to You. I am among the wrongdoers." And his saying, "If blessings had not come to him

from his Lord, he would have been thrown into the open air, and he is guilty." That is, if the mercy of Almighty God had not prevailed over him, as God moved and enabled him to repent. If you do this, he would have been expelled, that is, thrown out in the open, and would have been found guilty, but he would not have repented.

May God be pleased with him, he was thrown on the shore of the sea, and he was not to be blamed, but to be praised, so his Lord chose him, that is, he chose him for the second time after the first time, and he Made him one of the righteous, that is, among those prophets and messengers who were completely righteous, and this means that He chose him for the second time, because the first time He chose him when he was a messenger among the people of Nineveh and They had displeased him, so he left them out of boredom with them, so he was punished, and after chastisement and reproach. They recruited him again and after that interruption sent him back to his countrymen. Almighty God said from Surah Al-Yaqtin, "So We took him out into the open air when he was sick, and We made a tree grow over him." From a pumpkin, and we sent it to a million or more people, and they believed, so we gave them joy for a while

Ezikiel (Dhu al-Kifl)

Dhu al-Kifl (literally "Lord of the Part"; also spelled Dhu l-Kifl, Dhul-Kifl, Dhu al-Kifl, or Dhu l-Kifl) is an Islamic prophet. Although his identity is unknown, his have been identified with various Hebrew Bible prophets and other figures, most notably Ezekiel. Dhu al-Kifl is believed to have been elevated by Allah to a high position in life and is referred to in the Quran as "the company of the good". Although not much is known about Dhu al-Kifl from other historical sources, all the writings of classical commentators such as Ibn Ishaq and Ibn Kathir describe Dhu al-Kifl as a prophet, saintly figure. Who remained faithful in daily prayer and worship.

A mausoleum in the Ergani Province of Diyarbakir, Turkey, believed by some to be the resting place of the Prophet Dhu al-Kifl. It is situated on a hill called Maqam Daghi, 5 km from the city centre.

Ezekiel

Some believe that Dhu al-Kifl may be Ezekiel. When exile, monarchy and state were destroyed, political and national life was no longer possible. Corresponding to the two parts of his book, his personality and his preaching are alike dual, and the title Dhu al-Kifl means "the doubler" or "the adder".

Abdullah Yusuf Ali, in his Quranic commentary, says:
Dhu al-kifl would literally mean "possessing, or giving, double the reward or portion"; Or else, "one who used a cloak of double thickness," this is one of the meanings of kifal. Commentators differ on who is meant and why this title has been applied to him. I think the best suggestion is that given by Carsten Niebuhr in his Reisbeschreibung nach Arabia, Copenhagen, 1778, ii. 264–266, as cited in the Encyclopedia of Islam under Dhul-Kifl. He visited Meshad in Iraq, and also the small town of Kifl, midway between Najaf and Hilla (Babylon). He says that Kefil is the Arabic form of Ezekiel. Ezekiel's temple was there, and Jews came there on pilgrimage. If we consider "Dhu al-Kifl" not an adjective, but the Arabic form of "Ezekiel", then it fits the context, Ezekiel was a prophet in Israel whom Nebuchadnezzar took to Babylon after his second attack on Jerusalem. Was (about 599 BC). His book is included in the English Bible (Old Testament).
He was bound with chains, and thrown into prison, and for a time he became mute. He endured everything with patience and perseverance, and boldly rebuked the evils in Israel. In a fiery passage he condemns false leaders in words that are eternally true: "Woe to the shepherds of Israel who feed themselves! Shouldn't shepherds feed the sheep? You eat the fat, and you clothe yourself with the wool. Yes, kill those who eat, but do not feed the sheep. You have not strengthened the sick, nor healed the sick, nor bound up the broken..."

—Abdullah Yusuf Ali, The Holy Quran: Text, Translation and Commentary
Al Kifl) is a city in southeastern Iraq on the Euphrates River, between Najaf and Al Hilla. The shrine within Al Kifl has various names: Dhul Kifl Shrine, Markad Dhul Kifl, Qubbat Dhul Kifl, Qabr al-Nabi Dhu al-Kifl, Dhu al-Kifl Shrine, Dhu al-Kifl Shrine, Qabr Hazqiyal, Hazqiyil Shrine. Hazkiyal is the Arabic transliteration of the Hebrew Yehezkel, which was used mostly by Sephardi Jews after adopting Arabic. This

indicates that the Jews considered Ezekiel and Dhu al-Kifl to be identical, and Muslim interpreters also followed suit. Iraqi authorities claim that in 1316 (715–16 AH) the Ilkhanid Sultan Ulzaitu acquired guardianship rights over the tomb from the Jewish community.

As a result, the name of the temple was changed as per Islamic nomenclature for the same prophet. Sultan Uljaitu added to the structure by building a mosque and a minaret. He also renovated the temple, implementing some changes made evident by comparing its present state with the descriptions of pre-Ilkhanid travelers. The site remained a Muslim pilgrimage site until the early nineteenth century, when Menahim ibn Daniyal, a wealthy Jew, successfully converted it into a Jewish site and restored it. The minaret remains the only witness to its tenure as an Islamic site. Although the mosque and minaret were built in the 14th century, the antiquity of the temple and tomb cannot be determined.

in the Quran

Dhu al-Kifl is mentioned twice in the Quran in the following verses:

And remember Ishmael, Enoch, and Al-Kifl. They were all determined.

We included them in Our kindness, for they were truly among the righteous.

—Surah Al-Anbiya 21:85-86

Also remember Ishmael, Elisha and Zul-Kifl. All are among the best.

—Surah Sadh 38:48

In both cases, Dhu al-Kifl is mentioned in the context of the Quran's list of prophets, which also includes several others not mentioned in the verse quoted above.

The name Dhu al-Kifl literally means "owner of Kifl", using a type of name where ذُو Dhu ("owner of") is preceded by some specifically associated trait. Such names were used for other notable figures in the Quran, for example Dhu al-Qarnayn (Arabic: ذُو

ٱلْقَرْنَيْن, lit. 'He of the Two Horned/Two-Timed One'), and Dhu al-Nun (Arabic: ذُو ٱلنُّون, lit. 'the one with fish'), referring to Yunus. Kifal is an archaic Arabic word meaning "double" or "duplicate", originally meaning "to double" or "to multiply"; It was also used for folding clothes. The name is generally understood to mean "one of the dual parts". Some scholars have suggested that the name means "the one who receives double the reward" or rather "the one who received twice the reward", that is, it is a title for Job, as his family traces him back. Was done. According to the Quran and the Book of Job.

According to one view, it means "man of kifl", as "one of..." is another possible translation of the participle dhu, and kifl is reportedly the Arabic translation of "kapilvastu".

Dhu al-Kifal has also been identified with Joshua, Obadiah, and Isaiah. Or even Buddha.

Bible

Ezekiel 34:2-4

"Son of man, prophesy against the shepherds of Israel; Prophesy and say to them, This is what the Lord Jehovah says: Woe to you, you shepherds of Israel, who only care about yourselves! Shouldn't shepherds take care of the flock? You eat curd, wear wool, kill good animals, but do not take care of the sheep and goats. You neither strengthened the weak, nor healed the sick, nor bound the injured. You did not bring back the lost, nor did you seek the lost. You have ruled them harshly and cruelly.

Dr. Mustafa Khattab, The Clear Quran, 38:48 Footnote: "Scholars disagree as to whether ☐ul-Kifl was a prophet or just a righteous man. Those who agree that he was a prophet identify him in the Bible from various prophets such as Ezekiel, Isaiah, and Obadiah."

Yuksel, Edip; Al-Shayban, Layth Saleh; Schulte-Knafeh, Martha (2007). The Quran: A Reformed Translation. United States: Brainbow Press.

Remember Ishmael, Elisha and Isaiah; All are among the best. (38:48)

Is Dhul Kifl the same Gautam Buddha?

The Islamic prophet Dhu al-Kifal has been identified with the Buddha. The meaning of Dhu al-Kifl is still debated, but, according to this theory, it means "man of Kifl" and Kifl is the Arabic pronunciation of Kapilavastu, the city where the Buddha spent thirty years of his life. Another argument used by proponents of this theory is that the Buddha was from Kapil, the capital of a small kingdom located on the border of India and Nepal. He claims that Buddha not only belonged to Kapil, but was sometimes referred to as 'Kapil's'. This is exactly what the word 'Dhu al-Kifl' means. It should be remembered that the consonant 'pi' does not exist in Arabic and the closest consonant to it is 'fa'. Therefore, Kapil's name translated into Arabic becomes Kifl.

Proponents of this theory cite the first verses of the Quran's 95th chapter, Sura at-Tin:

From figs and olives, and from Mount Sinai, and from this safe city of Mecca!

—Quran, 95:1-3

Buddhist sources mention that Buddha attained enlightenment under a fig tree. So, according to the theory, from the places mentioned in these verses: Sinai is the place where Moses received revelation; Mecca is the place where Muhammad received revelation; And the olive tree is the place where Jesus received revelation. In this case, the remaining fig tree is the place where the Buddha received revelation.

Some[who?] take it a little further and say that Muhammad himself was a Buddha, since Buddha means "enlightened one".[citation needed]

Ahmadiyya sect

Mirza Tahir Ahmad, the fourth Caliph of the Ahmadiyya community, argues in his book Revelation, Rationality, Knowledge and Truth that the Buddha was actually a prophet of God who preached monotheism. He quoted from the inscriptions on the stupas of Ashoka which mention "Isana" which means God. He quotes, "Thus Devanampiya Piyadasi said: "Therefore from this time onwards, I have preached religious discourses, I have appointed religious rites, the hearing of which will bring mankind to walk on the right path , and will be given the glory of God* (Isāna)."Ahmadiyya believe that the Buddha was actually a prophet of God.

 Mirza Tahir Ahmed, in his book "An Elementary Study of Islam", also states that the Quranic figure named Dhul-Kifal may be the Buddha.

In fact, it is said in a verse of the Quran that God has sent many prophets to you (humanity). However, only a few have been named. Some people believe[who?] that the Buddha may (or may not) have been a prophet of God who taught monotheism to his people.

King David (Dawood)

According to Jewish works such as Seder Olam Rabbah, Seder Olam Zutta, and Sefer ha-Kabbalah (all written over a thousand years later), David ascended the throne as king of Judah in 885 BC. Tel Dan Stele, an Aramaic-written The stone, which was erected in the late 9th century BC/early 8th century BC by a king of Aram-Damascus to commemorate a victory over two enemy kings, contains the phrase Bytdwd (ᕗᕐᕗ ᑭᵐᕫ), which translates as "House". The Mesha Stele, built by King Mesha of Moab in the 9th century BC, may also refer to the "House of David", although this is disputed. Additionally, what little is known about David What is also known comes from Biblical literature, the historicity of which has been extensively challenged, and there is very little detail about David that is solid and undisputed.

In the Biblical narrative of the Books of Samuel, David is described as a young shepherd and harpist who gains fame by slaying Goliath. He becomes a favorite of Saul, the first king of Israel, but is forced to go into hiding when Saul suspects David is trying to take his throne. After Saul and his son Jonathan were killed in battle, David was appointed king by the tribe of Judah and eventually all the tribes of Israel. He conquers Jerusalem, makes it the capital of united Israel, and brings the Ark of the Covenant to the city. He commits adultery with Bathsheba and arranges the death of her husband, Uriah the Hittite. David's son Absalom later tries to overthrow him, but after Absalom's death David returns to Jerusalem to continue his rule. David wants to build a temple for Jehovah but is denied it because of the bloodshed during his reign. He dies at the age of 70 and chooses Bathsheba's son Solomon as his successor instead of his eldest son Adonijah. In Jewish prophetic literature David is revered as an ideal king and ancestor of the future Hebrew Messiah and several psalms are attributed to him.

David is also depicted extensively in post-biblical Jewish written and oral tradition and is referenced in the New Testament. Early Christians interpreted the life of Jesus of Nazareth in terms of the Hebrew Messiah and David; The Gospel of Matthew and the Gospel of Luke describe Jesus as a direct descendant of David. In the Quran and Hadith, David is described as an Israelite king as well as a prophet of Allah. The Biblical David has inspired many interpretations in art and literature over the centuries.

Both the First Book of Samuel and the First Book of Chronicles identify David as the son of the Bethlehemite Jesse, the youngest of eight sons. She also had at least two sisters: Zeruiah, whose sons all went on to serve in David's army, and Abigail, whose son Amasa served in Absalom's army, Absalom being one of David's younger sons. While the Bible does not name her mother, the Talmud identifies her as Nitzvet, the daughter of a man named Adel, and in the Book of Ruth she is claimed by Boaz as the great-grandson of Ruth the Moabite. .

David is described as having strengthened his ties with various political and national groups through marriage. According to 1 Samuel 17:25, King Saul said that whoever killed Goliath would make him a very rich man, give him his daughter and declare his father's family exempt from taxes in Israel. Saul offered David his eldest daughter Merab in marriage, which David respectfully declined. Then Saul married Merab to Adriel from Maholah. Upon being told that his younger daughter Michal was in love with David, Saul married her to David in exchange for payment for Philistine skins. Saul became jealous of David and tried to kill him. David ran away. Then Saul sent Galim to marry Michael to Palti, son of Laish. According to 2 Samuel 3, David took wives in Hebron; They were Ahinoam the Jezreelite; Abigail, widow of Nabal of Carmel; Maacah, daughter of Talme, king of Geshur; Haggith; Abital; And Agla. Later, David wanted Michal back and Ish-Bosheth's commander Abner handed him over to him, much to Palti's chagrin.

The Book of Chronicles lists his sons along with their various wives and concubines. In Hebron, David had six sons: Amnon, from Ahinoam; Daniel, by Abigail; Absalom, by Makah; Adonijah, by Hagith; Shephatiah, by Abital; and Ithrim, by Eglah. His sons from Bathsheba were Shammu, Shobab, Nathan and Solomon. Sons born in Jerusalem by David's other wives included Ibar, Elishua, Eliphalet, Noga, Nepheg, Japhiah, Elishama, and Eliada. Jerimoth, who is not mentioned in any genealogy, is mentioned as another of his sons in 2 Chronicles 11:18. Maachah's daughter Tamar is raped by her half-brother Amnon. David fails to bring Amnon to justice for his violation of Tamar, as he is his first child and he loves her, and so Absalom (his full brother) murders Amnon to avenge Tamar. Despite the great sins they had committed, David expressed grief over the deaths of his sons, weeping twice for Amnon [2 Samuel 13:31-26] and seven times for Absalom.

Asr al-Tafsir's interpretation of the words of Abu Bakr al-Jazairi

17 Night Trip 55

Abu Bakr al-Jazairi (born 1921 AD) (died 2018 AD)

Word Explanation:

Which is better: i.e. the word which is better than others because of its kindness and beauty.

This leads to corruption in them.

Clear Enemy: Means clear enmity.

Your Lord knows best about you: this is the word that is best.

And We have not sent you as a guardian over them, that is, you should force them to believe.

We favored some prophets: that is, by distinguishing each of them with his own qualities.

And We gave David the Psalms: that is, a book which is a Psalm. This is a kind of priority.

Meaning of the verse:

The context is still in seeking guidance for the people of Mecca, through dialogue and debate, and it happened that some of the believers confronted some of the unbelievers during the debate with harsh words, as if threatening them with the torment of the Fire. This aroused the ire of the polytheists, so God Almighty commanded His Messenger to say to the believers, when they address the polytheists, not to speak harshly to them, so God Almighty said: { And say to My servants, that is, the believers, "Say that which is best" of words, so that they may find a way to the hearts of the unbelievers. And God Almighty gave a reason for that, saying, "Indeed, Satan stirs up among them," the whisper, and spoils the relationships that could have been achieved in guiding the lost, and that is because Satan was and still is. Man has an enemy Making clear, that is, he made clear the apparent enmity, as he does not want the infidel to convert to Islam, and does not want the Muslim to be rewarded and rewarded for his call. And God Almighty says: {Your Lord is most knowledgeable of you. If He wills, He would have mercy on you} Then He will turn to you, so you will submit. {Or if He willed, He could punish you} by leaving you to die as a result of your polytheism, so you would enter the Fire. Such words should be said by the believers to the unbelievers, not to pass judgment on them that they are the people of Hell and will remain therein forever. This would annoy the polytheists and they would persist in stubbornness and arrogance. And God Almighty says: {And We have not sent you as a guardian over them}. God Almighty says to His Messenger, "Indeed, we did not send you as a watchdog over them so that you could force them to convert to Islam. Rather, we sent you to convey Our call to them in a good manner and to guide them to us." In this, we teach the believers how to call the unbelievers to Islam. And God Almighty says: {And your Lord knows best of those who are in the heavens and the earth} God Almighty tells His Messenger and the believers implicitly that God Almighty knows best who is in the heavens and the earth, let alone these polytheists. He knows best what is best for them and knows best what has been written for them or upon them of happiness or misery, and the reasons for that of faith or disbelief, and accordingly. So do not grieve over their denial, do not despair of their faith, and do not burden yourself with what you cannot bear to guide them, so say that which is best, and leave the matter of guiding them to God Almighty. He is their Lord and most knowledgeable of them, and His Almighty says: {And We have favored some of the prophets over others, and We gave David a Psalm.} God Almighty tells of His blessings among His servants So the one who excelled among the prophets, and he is the most perfect of creation and the purest of them, this is his virtue by virtue, like Abraham, and this is by speech, like Moses, and this is by the book full of praises, praises, lessons, and sermons, like David, and you, O Muhammad, by forgiving you of your previous and future sins, and by sending you to all people and other blessings, and if this truth becomes clear, You know that God knows best who deserves guidance and who deserves to go astray, as well as mercy and torment, so entrust the matter to Him, and call upon His servants with kindness and gentleness and with words that are better than other words.

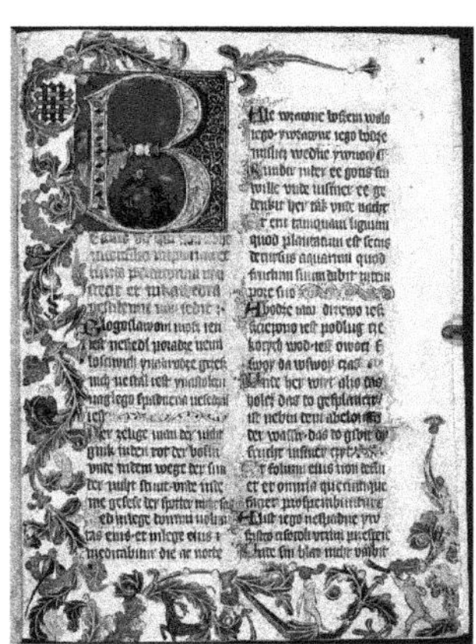

King Solomon (Sulaiman)

Solomon, also known as Jedidiah, was a king of ancient Israel and the son and successor of King David, according to the Hebrew Bible and the Old Testament. He is described as the joint ruler of Israel and Judah. The approximate dates of Solomon's reign are 970–931 BC. After his death, his son and successor Rehoboam pursued a harsh policy towards the northern tribes, ultimately leading to the division of the Israelites between the Kingdom of Israel in the north and the Kingdom of Judah in the south. After the division, his patrilineal descendants ruled Judah alone.

The Bible says that Solomon built the first temple in Jerusalem, this temple was dedicated to Jehovah, or God in Judaism. Solomon is portrayed as wealthy, wise, and powerful, and one of the 48 Jewish prophets. He is also the subject of numerous later references and legends, notably in the Testament of Solomon (part of the 1st century Biblical Apocrypha).

However there is no mention of Solomon in that time period. Apart from scriptures written later, no contemporary archaeological evidence has been found to indicate that it existed.

In the New Testament, he is portrayed as a teacher of excellent wisdom by Jesus of Nazareth, and adorned with glory but excelled by the "lily of the field". He is considered a major Islamic prophet in the Quran. In most non-Biblical circles, Solomon also became known as a magician and exorcist, with his name mentioned in many amulets and medallion seals from the Hellenistic period.

Solomon's life is described primarily in 2 Samuel, 1 Kings, and 2 Chronicles. His two names mean "peaceful" and "friend of God", both of which are considered "prophetic of the character of his reign".

Rabbinical tradition attributes the Book of Wisdom (contained within the Septuagint) to Solomon, although the book was probably written in the 2nd century BCE. In this work, Solomon is portrayed as an astronomer. [Where?] His name also appears in other books of wisdom poetry such as Odes of Solomon and Psalms of Solomon. The Jewish historian Eupolemus, who wrote about 157 BC, included copies of apocryphal letters exchanged between Solomon and the kings of Egypt and Tyre.
The Gnostic Apocalypse of Adam, which may date from the first or second century, refers to a legend in which Solomon sent an army of demons to seek out a virgin girl who had fled from him, perhaps the most common of the later stories. The first surviving mention is of Solomon subduing demons and making them his slaves. This tradition of Solomon's control over demons appears in full detail in the early pseudo-epigraphic work called the Testament of Solomon, with its detailed and bizarre demonology.

Temple Mount in Jerusalem

Very little archaeological excavation has been conducted around the area known as the Temple Mount, believed to be the foundation of Solomon's Temple, because efforts to do so have met with opposition by Muslim officials of the Jerusalem Waqf.

precious metals from tarshish

Biblical passages that understand Tarshish as the source of King Solomon's great wealth of metals – especially silver, but also gold, tin and iron (Ezekiel 27) – are echoed by archaeological evidence of silver deposits found in Phenicia in 2013. Were connected to. Tarshish was reportedly obtained by Solomon in partnership with King Hiram of Phoenician Tire (Isaiah 23) and the fleet of Tarshish and the ships that operated in his service. The silver deposits provide the first recognized physical evidence that matches ancient texts relating to Solomon's kingdom and his wealth (see 'Wealth' above).

<u>In Islamic tradition</u>, Solomon is also known as Suleiman ibn Dawud, and is recognized as a prophet and messenger of God, as well as a divinely appointed king. Solomon inherited his position as the prophet king of the Israelites from his father. Contrary to the Bible, according to Muslim tradition, Solomon himself never participated in idolatry, but was rebuked for allowing it in his kingdom.

The Quran ascribes to Solomon a great level of knowledge, wisdom and power. He knew the language of birds (Romani: maniq al-ayyar).
In Islam Solomon was also known to have other God-given supernatural abilities, such as controlling the wind, ruling over the jinn, enslaving the gods, and hearing the conversations of ants:

And We made the wind subservient to Solomon; His morning walk was for a month, and his evening walk was also for a month. And We sent down for him a stream of molten copper, and We subjected some of the jinn to serve him by the will of his Lord.

And those among them who deviated from Our Command, We made them taste the punishment of the Fire.

—Surah Sabah 34:12

And when they reached a valley of ants, an ant warned, "O ants! Go quickly to your homes lest Solomon and his armies crush you unawares."

—Surah An-Namal 27:18-19
The Quran absolves Solomon from practicing witchcraft:
Instead they followed the magic promoted by the devils during the reign of Solomon. Solomon never disbelieved, but the devils disbelieved. They taught the people magic, as well as what was revealed to the two angels, Harut and Marut.

In Babylon. The two angels never taught anyone except saying, "We are only a test for you, so do not abandon your faith." Yet people learned magic which created a rift between husband and wife; However their magic could not harm anyone except by the will of Allah. They learned what harmed them and what did not benefit them – although they already knew that whoever bought magic would have no share in the Hereafter. Miserable indeed was the price for which they sold their souls, if they only knew!

—Surah Al-Baqarah 2:102
The Quran refers to a "puppet" personified as Solomon, understood in foreign literature as a jinni or demon, who escaped from captivity and took over his kingdom. Solomon losing his throne to demons is understood in Islamic spirituality to be a human being losing his soul due to demonic obsession.

The Attar of Nishapur writes: "If you bind Div (the demon), you will leave for the royal pavilion with Solomon" and "You have no control over your kingdom, because in your case Div is in place of Solomon. "

The gifts of Solomon are often used as a metaphor in popular literature. The demons taking over Solomon's kingdom reflects the Sufi concept of succumbing to the evil desires of the mind. The ant is depicted as an intelligent creature, who tells Solomon the reason behind her gift of controlling the wind and her name.

During the Islamization of Iran, Solomon became merged with Jamshid, a legendary king from Persian mythology who is ascribed similar qualities.

In the Bahá'í Faith, Solomon is considered one of the minor prophets, along with David, Isaiah, Jeremiah, Ezekiel, and others. Bahá'ís view Solomon as a prophet sent by God to address the issues of his time. Bahá'u'lláh wrote about Solomon in Hidden Words. He is also mentioned by Solomon in the Tablet of Wisdom, where he is depicted as a contemporary of Pythagoras.
fables

angels and magic

According to rabbinic literature, only because of his humble request for knowledge, Solomon was rewarded with wealth and an unprecedented glorious realm, extending to the entire terrestrial world, including the upper world inhabited by angels and all its inhabitants. All animals, birds, reptiles, as well as demons and spirits. His control over demons, spirits and animals enhanced his splendor, with demons bringing him precious stones, as well as water from distant lands to irrigate his exotic plants. Animals and birds entered the kitchen of Solomon's palace willingly, so that they could be used as food for him, and extravagant meals were prepared for him daily by each of his 700 wives and 300 concubines, this With the thought that perhaps the king would host a feast in his house that day.

<u>The Seal of Solomon</u> is the legendary signet ring given to Solomon in medieval mystical traditions, from which it developed in parallel with Jewish mysticism, Islamic mysticism, and Western occultism. It is the predecessor to the Star of David, a contemporary cultural and religious symbol of the Jewish people. It was often depicted in the shape of a pentagram or hexagram. In religious legends, the ring is described as having given Solomon the power to give supernatural commands and also the ability to talk to animals. Due to the cosmic Wisdom of Solomon, it came to be seen as an amulet or talisman, or a symbol or character in medieval magic and Renaissance magic, magic and alchemy.

Solomon and Asmodeus

 The story of King Solomon and Ashmedai) tells that Solomon one day asked Asmodeus how demons could be made powerful over man, and Asmodeus asked him to free him and give him the ring so that he could demonstrate; Solomon agreed but Asmodeus threw the ring into the sea and it was swallowed by a fish. Then Asmodeus swallowed the king, stood fully erect with one wing touching heaven and the earth with the other, and spat out Solomon a distance of 400 miles. The rabbis claim that this was a divine punishment for Solomon's failure to obey three divine commandments, and Solomon was forced to wander from city to city, until he eventually came to an Ammonite city. Reached where he was forced to work in the king's kitchen. Solomon had the opportunity to prepare a meal for the Ammonite king, which the king found so impressive that the previous cook was dismissed and Solomon was put in his place; The king's daughter, Naamah, later fell in love with Solomon, but the family (thinking Solomon was a commoner) disapproved, so the king decided to kill them both by sending them into the desert. Solomon and the king's daughter wandered through the desert until they reached a coastal town, where they bought a fish to eat, which happened to be the same fish that had swallowed the magic ring. Solomon was then able to reclaim his throne and expel Asmodeus. The element of the ring being thrown into the sea and recovered in the stomach of a fish also appeared in Herodotus's account of Polycrates, tyrant of Samos (circa 538–522 BC).

In another familiar version of the legend of the Seal of Solomon, Asmodeus disguises himself. In some myths, he is disguised as King Solomon himself. The hidden Asmodeus tells travelers who have traveled to King Solomon's magnificent high palace that the Seal of Solomon was thrown into the sea. He then convinces them to land in it and attempt to retrieve it, because if they do so he will take the throne as king.

in Kabbalah

Early followers of Kabbalah depicted Solomon flying in the air on a throne of light placed on an eagle, which brought him to the heavenly gates as well as to the dark mountains, behind which were chained the fallen angels Uzza and Azazel; The eagle would rest on chains, and Solomon, using the magic ring, would force the two angels to reveal every secret he wanted to know.

castle without entrance

According to one legend, while making a magical journey, Solomon saw a magnificent palace with no entrance. He ordered the demons to climb onto the roof and see if they could find any living creatures within the building, but all they found was an eagle, which he said was 700 years old, but he had never seen the entrance. . Then an elder brother of Baz, who was 900 years old, was found, but he too did not know the entrance. The eldest brother of these two birds, who was 1,300 years old, then announced that his father had informed him that the door was to the west, but that it was hidden by wind-swept sand. Upon discovering the entrance, Solomon found a statue inside with a silver tablet in its mouth saying in Greek (a language that modern scholars had not thought to exist for 1000 years)

Before the time of Solomon) that the idol was Shaddad, son of 'Aad, and he ruled over a million cities, rode on a million horses, had a million vassals under him and killed a million warriors, then Yet she could not resist the angel of death.

The throne of Solomon is described in detail in Targum Sheni, compiled from three different sources, and in two later Midrash. According to these, there were twelve golden lions on the steps of the throne, each facing a golden eagle. The throne had six steps, on which animals, all of gold, were arranged in the following order: a lion in front of a bull on the first step; on another, a wolf opposite a sheep; on the third, a tiger opposite a camel; on the fourth, an eagle in front of a peacock, on the fifth, a cat in front of a rooster; On the sixth, a sparrow-hawk opposite a dove. At the top of the throne was a dove holding a sparrow-hawk in its talons, symbolizing Israel's dominance over the Gentiles. The first Midrash claims that the six stairs were built because Solomon prophesied that six kings would sit on the throne, namely Solomon, Rehoboam, Hezekiah,

Manasseh, Amon, and Josiah. There was also a golden candlestick at the top of the throne, with the names of the seven patriarchs Adam, Noah, Shem, Abraham, Isaac, Jacob and Job engraved on its seven branches on one side, and Levi, Kohath, Amram, Moses on the seven others. , Aaron, Eldad, Medad and also the names of Hur (another version has Haggai). Above the candelabrum was a golden jar filled with olive oil and below that was a golden basin that supplied the jar with oil and on which were engraved the names of Nadab, Abihu and Eli and his two sons. Above the throne, twenty-four vines were planted to shade the king's head.

Sulayman ibn Dawud, lit. 'Solomon son of David'), according to the Quran, was a Malik (مَلِك, lit. 'king') and Nabi (نَبِيّ, lit. 'prophet') of the Israelites. Generally, Islamic tradition holds that he was the third king of Israel and a wise ruler.

<u>In Islam,</u> Solomon is considered one of God's prophets, who was given many divine gifts, including the ability to speak to both animals and jinn; He is also said to have enslaved Shayatin (شياتين, literally 'devil') and Div (ديو, literally 'demon') with the help of a rod or ring given to him by God.

Muslims further say that he remained a faithful monotheist throughout his life; Reigned with justice over the entire nation of Israel; He attained a level of kingship that was not given to anyone before him or after him; And at the end of his life he fulfilled all his commandments, promising closeness to God in Jannah (جَنَّة, literally 'paradise'). Since the rise of Islam, various Muslim historians have considered Solomon to be one of the greatest rulers in history.

Solomon and Ifrit

When Bilqis was on her way to Solomon's court, the king asked his servants to hand over his throne before her arrival. An Ifrit offered his services (27:38–40), but Solomon declined, and entrusted the task to a servant, named in traditions as Asif ibn Barakhiya. Being a pious man, the servant prayed to God to transfer the throne to him. Their prayers were answered, by the power of God the throne appeared in Solomon's palace. When Bilqis arrived, Solomon asked her if she recognized his throne. Struggling to understand the miracle performed by God, he at first gave an evasive answer to the king, but later adopted Solomon's faith, won over by evidence that the miracle was not of Ifrit alone but of God himself. Solomon had rejected Ifrit's attractive offer, because he wanted to trust completely in God, not a demon or any other created being, and was successful in converting Bilqis to the true faith because of his piety. He was rewarded for it.

Death

The Quran tells that Solomon died while he was leaning on his staff and he remained standing, leaning on it, until a small creature – an ant or a worm – gnawed at him, until, eventually, he gave way. Did not give - and only then did he die from body collapse.

When We ordered the death of Solomon, the jinn did not receive any sign that he was dead except that termites ate his staff. So when he fell, the jinn realized that if they had truly known the Invisible, they would not have lived in such humiliating slavery.

—Surah Sabah 34:14

Since he was standing upright with the support of his stick, the genie thought he was still alive and watching over them.

They realized the truth when God sent a creature to crawl out of the ground and gnaw at Solomon's staff until its body collapsed. This verse is understood to teach the audience that the jinn do not know the unseen (al-Ghaib) – if they knew it, they would not labor like fools in the service of a dead person.

According to Shahnama of poet Firdausi, Amshid was the fourth king of the world. It is believed that, like Solomon, he had control over all the angels and demons in the world, and was both king and high priest of Hormozd (Middle Persian for Ahura Mazda). He was responsible for many great inventions that made the lives of his people more secure: the manufacturing of armor and weapons, the weaving and dyeing of linen, silk and wool fabrics, the construction of brick houses, the mining of jewelry and precious metals. , perfume and wine making, the art of medicine, navigation of the waters of the world in sailing ships. That Jamshed had now become the greatest emperor the world had ever seen. He was endowed with royal fur (Avestan: khvarena), a bright splendor burning all around him by divine grace.

Due to the similarity between the two wise kings, some traditions conflate the two. For example, the works of Sulayman al-Balkhi were associated with ruling south-western Iran. Persepolis is believed to have been the seat of Solomon and scholars such as Masoudi, Muqaddasi and Istakhri called it "Solomon's playground". Other Muslim writers have contested the notion that Solomon once ruled in Iran Persia, arguing that any resemblance between the lives and works of Solomon and Jamshid is entirely coincidental, the two being distinct and separate personalities. . The latter view has been upheld by scholarship in the field of Indo-European mythology, which has conclusively demonstrated that the character of Jamshid is derived from the early Zoroastrian deity Yima, while Quranic and Biblical scholarship has to some extent disputed the historicity. supports. Wise prophet king.

Tafsir

21 Al-Anbiyâ' (81 الأنبياء)

Tanwîr al-Miqbâs min Tafsîr Ibn 'Abbâs

* تفسير Tanwîr al-Miqbâs min Tafsîr Ibn 'Abbâs
(And unto Solomon (We subdued) the wind in its raging. It set by His command) and it is also said that this means: by Solomon's command (towards the land which We had blessed) with water and trees; this is the Holy Land: Jordan and Palestine. (And of everything) We subdued for him (We are aware).

Tafsir Ibn 'Abbâs, trans. Mokrane Guezzou
Royal Aal al-Bayt Institute for Islamic Thought, Amman, Jordan

21 Al-Anbiyâ' (الأنبياء)
82

Tafsir al-Jalalayn

* تفسير Tafsir al-Jalalayn

And We disposed of the devils some that dived for him plunging into the sea and bringing out of it jewels for Solomon and performed tasks other than that that is other than diving such as building and otherwise. And We were watchful over them lest they should spoil what they had made for whenever they completed a task before nightfall they would invariably spoil it unless they were occupied with some other task.

Tafsir al-Jalalayn, trans. Feras Hamza
Royal Aal al-Bayt Institute for Islamic Thought, Amman, Jordan .

Tafsir ahsanul bayan

27:16

And David was succeeded by Solomon (1) and he said, O people! We have been taught the language of birds (2) and everything has been given to us (3) Verily, this is the open grace of God.

16.1 This refers to the inheritance of prophecy and kingship, of which only Solomon (peace be upon him) was declared the heir. Otherwise, Hazrat Dawood (peace be upon him) had other sons who were deprived of their inheritance. However, the legacy of the prophets is in knowledge, the wealth they leave behind is charity, as the Prophet (peace and blessings of Allah be upon him) said (al-Bukhari, Kitab al-Fariz wa Muslim, Kitab al-Jihad).

16.2 All animals were taught dialects, but birds are especially mentioned because they always huddled together for shade. And some people say that only the dialects of birds were taught and that the beaks also belong to birds. (Fatahul-Qadir)

16.3 What did they want, such as knowledge, prophethood, intelligence, wealth, jinn and humans, birds and animals, etc.

Tafsir Jalalain

34:14

And when We decreed death for him, for Solomon, in other words, [when] he died – he stood with his staff supported for a whole year, while the jinn continued to toil as was customary, until his death. Unaware, until [finally] a termite ate his stick, he fell to the ground [and it was seen] that he died – they found nothing except the termites to indicate that he had died (Al-Ard Uridath The verbal noun from al is -khashaaba, passive verbal form, in other words, 'It [the piece of wood] was eaten away by the termites [al-arada]') which gnawed away at its staff (read minsa'atahu or minstahu, hamza) An alif, meaning 'staff', is so called because [when describing it one would say] yunus'u bih, meaning it is used to repel or drive away [creatures] is done'). And when he fell down, died, the jinn realized, it became clear to them, that (one, has become soft, in other words, Annahum) did they know the invisible - in which they were revealed in the way of Solomon was hidden dead - They did not continue [in which they continued] in the humiliating chastisement, in the hard labor, because they believed that He was alive, which is contrary to what they would have expected if they had known the unseen and the fact that that he lived there for a full year, given how many of his servants were eaten by termites after his death; In other words, [they are not able to continue the humiliating chastisement for [more] than a day or even a night.

Tafsir ahsanul bayan

38:34

And We tested Solomon (peace and blessings of Allaah be upon him) and placed a corpse on his throne, then (1) it turned back.

34.1 What kind of case was this, how was the dead body kept on the chair? And what does that mean? There is no description of this in the Holy Quran or Hadith. However, some commentators have associated with it an incident proven by Sahih Hadith, and that is that Hazrat Sulaiman (peace be upon him) once said that I will kill all my wives tonight (whose number was 70 or 90). Slept with. I'll do that. So that from them are born kings who fight in the path of Allah. And he did not say 'Inshallah' (i.e. trusted only in his plan) and the result was that none of his wives became pregnant except one. And the child the pregnant wife gave birth to was defective i.e. half the child. The Prophet (peace and blessings of Allaah be upon him) said, "If Sulayman (peace and blessings of Allaah be upon him) had said, 'Inshallah, then all Mujahids would have been born' (Sahih Bukhari).

Elijah (Ilyas)

Ilyas was a prophet and messenger of God (Allah) who was sent to guide the Children of Israel. He was given the prophetic mission to stop people from worshiping idols. Ilyas is the prophetic predecessor of Alyasa. Some Islamic scholars believe that Ilyas is from the descendants of Harun (Aaron).

early life

In Islamic sources, Ilyas' full name is Ilyas ibn Yasin.

According to many Islamic sources and the Bible, Ilyas is alive and has ascended to the sky. However, Ibn Kathir did not accept these hadiths and considered them among the Israelites. In Mu'azm al-Buldan, Yaqut al-Hamawi mentions a tomb for Ilyas at Baalbek. A temple was later built over this grave, but it was dedicated to the "Prophet Aila", although the locals believed that it was the grave of Elias.

Quran

Elijah is mentioned in the Quran, where his sermon is narrated in a concise manner. The Quran tells that Elijah told his people to worship God and abandon the worship of Baal, the primary idol of the region. The Quran says:

"Indeed Elijah was one of the apostles. When he said to his people: "Will you not fear God? "Will you call upon Baal and forsake the best Creator, God, your Lord and Sustainer and the Lord and Sustainer of your ancient ancestors?

—As-Safat 123–126

The Quran makes it clear that the majority of Elijah's people rejected the Prophet and continued to practice idolatry. However, it mentions that a small number of them followed God's dedicated servant Elijah and believed in God and worshiped him. The Quran states, "They denied him (Elijah), and surely they will be punished, except the honest and devoted servants of God (among them). And We have enshrined him (the memory) for generations to come." Left it."

In the Quran, God praises Elijah in two places:

Peace be upon Eliza! This is how We reward those who do good. He is truly one of our faithful servants.
—Quran, Chapter 37 (As-Safat), verses 129-132[

And Zachariah and Yahya and Isa and Elijah, they were all among the righteous.

—Quran, Chapter 6 (al-Anām), verse 85
Several commentators, including Abdullah Yusuf Ali, commenting on verse 85, have said that Elijah, Zakariya, Yahya and Isa were all spiritually connected. Abdullah Yusuf Ali says, "The third group are not people of action, but preachers of the truth, who lead solitary lives. Their adjective is: "The righteous." They form a close-knit group around Jesus. Zachariah The father of John was the Baptist, who is referred to as "Elijah, who was to come" (Matthew 11:14); and Elijah is said to have been present and spoke to Jesus at the Transfiguration on the Mount (Matthew 17:3)."

Although most Muslim scholars believed that Elijah preached in Israel, some early commentators on the Quran said that Elijah was sent to Baalbek in Lebanon. Modern scholars have rejected this claim, stating that the city's association with Elijah may have stemmed from the first part of the city's name being Baal, the god whom Elijah encouraged his people to stop worshiping. did. Scholars who refuse to identify Elijah's city with Baalbek further argue that the city of Baalbek is not mentioned in association with the story of Elijah in the Quran or the Hebrew Bible.

death

As time passed, drought spread and many people died. When they saw themselves being tortured, they regretted their past actions, turned to Ilyas and accepted his invitation. Then, due to the prayers of Ilyas, it rained heavily and the land was satisfied; However, after some time, people forgot their covenant with God and turned to idol worship. When Ilyas saw this, he asked God for his death; But, God sent a chariot of fire for him and he ascended into the sky and chose Elisa, who was his disciple, as his deputy. Ilyas is rarely associated with Islamic eschatology. However, some Muslims believe that Ilyas is expected to return during the end times along with the mysterious figure Khidr.

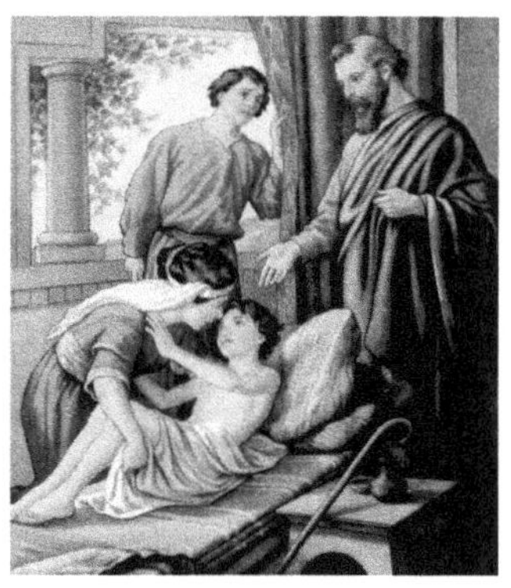

Elisha (Aliasa)

Alyssa is a prophet and messenger of Allah who was sent to guide the Children of Israel. In the Quran, Alyssa is mentioned twice as a great prophet, and both times is mentioned along with the companion prophets. He is revered by Muslims as the prophetic successor of Ilyas (Elijah). Islamic sources identifying Elisha with Khidr cite the strong relationship between Khidr and Ilyas in Islamic tradition.

Alyasa's name is mentioned twice in Al-Anam 6:86 and Saad 38:48. In those verses, without mentioning anything about Aliyāsa's personality or prophethood, he is mentioned as "graceful" and "among the chosen ones." According to the Quran, Elisha is considered "above the rest of creation" and is "among the most excellent" (l-akhyar). Alyasa is mentioned along with Ismail in al-An'am 6:86 and Sa'd 38:48:

Luqman

Luqman is often identified with the fabulist and storyteller Aesop, whose fables are found in many ancient cultures. Sometime during the Middle Ages, much of what was said about Aesop in Europe was transmitted to Luqman. This identification with Aesop is confirmed by the fact that many of the fables associated with Aesop in the West are related to Luqman in the East.

An Arab mythological figure named 'Luqman' also existed long before the figure of the wise 'Luqman' appeared in the Quran, resulting in considerable debate of theological and historical nature regarding the relationship of the two characters. Some, such as the 17th-century French scholar Pierre-Daniel Huet, say that the two are the same person, but others argue that they simply have the same name. In Arabic proverb collections, the two characters are conflated, taken from both the Quran and pre-Islamic stories, attributing supernatural powers and lifespan to Luqman. Pre-Islamic Luqman was among the Ad people, who lived in the Arabian Peninsula near modern-day Yemen.

Lived in Al-Ahqaf. Luqman (Entity of the Quran) is from Nubia, more recently Sudan. The Luqman mentioned in the Quran is Nubian and not Mediterranean.

Source of Luqman's Wisdom

According to the 12th verse of Surah Luqman in the Quran, Luqman was given knowledge by God, Al-Hakim (The Most Wise).

We gave wisdom to Luqman, and said, "Be grateful to God", and whoever is grateful is truly grateful for his benefit, and whoever is ungrateful, then God is free from all needs, worthy of all praise. Is.

—Surah Luqman Quran 31:12
According to a hadith in the Muwatta of Imam Malik, Luqman was asked, referring to his high position, "What has brought you to what we see?" Luqman said, "True speech, fulfilling the faith, and leaving aside what does not concern me." Hakam who heard it from Umar ibn Qays.

In another Hadith it is stated that a high position in Paradise has been prescribed for some people. However, when the person has not earned good karma to reach that high position, God gives him certain tests or examinations which, if accepted and patiently endured, will lead to a higher position. .

Luqman was captured by slavers and sold as a slave. He was deprived of his freedom and could neither move nor speak freely. However, he suffered his bondage patiently, faithfully, and hopefully, waiting for God's action. This was the first of the trials that he had to bear.

The man who bought Luqman was good-hearted and intelligent, treating Luqman with kindness. He was able to detect that Luqman was not ordinary and thus, tried to test his intelligence and discovered its reality.

One day, the man ordered Luqman to slaughter a sheep and Luqman slaughtered the sheep. Then, he ordered Luqman to bring its best parts to him and Luqman took its heart and tongue to his master. On receiving them, his master smiled, fascinated by

Luqman's choice of the 'best' part of the sheep. He understood that Luqman was trying to convey some deep meaning, even though he could not determine exactly what. From that moment onwards, his owner began to take more interest in Luqman and became kinder to him than before.

A few days later, Luqman was again instructed to slaughter a sheep - which he did - but this time he was asked to take the worst parts of the animal to his master. Once again, Luqman brought the heart and the tongue - to his master's amazement. When the master mentioned this to Luqman, the wise Luqman answered, "The tongue and the heart are the sweetest parts if they are good, and nothing can be worse than these if they are wicked!"after that, Luqman's owner held him in great respect. Many people consulted Luqman for advice, and the fame of his wisdom spread all over the country. Such was the knowledge of Luqman Al-Hakim.

Tafsir ibne kathir

31:12

Luqman

The Salaf differed over the identity of Luqman; there are two opinions:

was he a Prophet or
just a righteous servant of Allah without the Prophethood.

The majority favored the latter view, that he was a righteous servant of Allah without being a Prophet.

Sufyan Ath-Thawri said, narrating from Al-Ash`ath, from Ikrimah, from Ibn Abbas,

"Luqman was an Ethiopian slave who was a carpenter.

Abdullah bin Az-Zubayr said,

"I said to Jabir bin Abdullah:`What did you hear about Luqman?'

He said:`He was short with a flat nose, and came from Nubia.'"

Yahya bin Sa`id Al-Ansari narrated from Sa`id bin Al-Musayyib that

"Luqman was from the black peoples of (southern) Egypt, and had thick lips. Allah gave him wisdom but withheld Prophethood from him."

Al-Awza`i said,

"Abdur-Rahman bin Harmalah told me; `A black man came to Sa`id bin Al-Musayyib to ask him a question, and Sa`id bin Al-Musayyib said to him:

"Do not be upset because you are black, for among the best of people were three who were black:Bilal, Mahja` the freed slave of Umar bin Al-Khattab, and Luqman the Wise, who was a black Nubian with thick lips."

Ibn Jarir recorded that Khalid Ar-Raba`i said:

"Luqman was an Ethiopian slave who was a carpenter. His master said to him, `Slaughter this sheep for us,' so he slaughtered it.

(His master) said:`Bring the best two pieces from it,' so he brought out the tongue and the heart.

Then time passed, as much as Allah willed, and (his master) said:`Slaughter this sheep for us,' so he slaughtered it.

(His master) said, 'Bring the worst two morsels from it,' so he brought out the tongue and the heart.

His master said to him, 'I told you to bring out the best two pieces, and you brought these, then I told you to bring out the worst two pieces, and you brought these!'

Luqman said,

'There is nothing better than these if they are good, and there is nothing worse than these if they are bad.'"

Shu'bah narrated from Al-Hakam, from Mujahid,

"Luqman was a righteous servant, but he was not a Prophet."

Allah's saying:

And indeed We bestowed upon Luqman Al-Hikmah,

means, understanding, knowledge and eloquence.

saying:"Give thanks to Allah."

means, 'We commanded him to give thanks to Allah for the blessings and favors that Allah had given to him alone among his people and contemporaries.'

Then Allah says:

And whoever gives thanks, he gives thanks for (the good of) himself.

meaning, the benefit of that will come back to him, and Allah's reward is for those who give thanks, as He says:

and whosoever does righteous good deeds, then such will prepare a good place for themselves. (30:44)

And whoever is unthankful, then verily, Allah is Rich, Worthy of all praise.

He has no need of His servants and He will not be harmed by that, even if all the people of the earth were to disbelieve, for He has no need of anything or anyone besides Himself.

There is no God but He, and we worship none but Him

Zachariah (Zakaria)

According to the Quran, 1-Zakariya was said to be a priest and prophet of God whose office was in the Second Temple in Jerusalem. He was often in charge of managing the temple services 2 -and he was always steadfast in prayer to the Lord.

Praying for a son
As he reached his old age, Zakariya began to worry over who would continue the legacy of preaching the message of God after his death and who would carry on the daily services of the temple after him. Zakariya started to pray to God for a son. The praying for the birth of an offspring was not merely out of the desire for a child. He prayed both for himself and for the public – they needed a messenger, a man of God who would work in the service of the Lord after Zakariya. Zakariya had character and virtue and he wanted to transfer this to his spiritual heir as his most precious possession. His dream was to restore the household to the posterity of the Patriarch Jacob, and to make sure the message of God was renewed for Israel. As the Qur'an recounts:

19:4 saying, "My Lord! Surely my bones have become brittle, and grey hair has spread across my head, but I have never been disappointed in my prayer to You, my Lord!
19:5 And I am concerned about ˹the faith of˺ my relatives after me, since my wife is barren. So grant me, by Your grace, an heir,

19:6 who will inherit ˹prophethood˺ from me and the family of Jacob, and make him, O Lord, pleasing ˹to You˺!"

—Surah Maryam 19:4-6

Fathering Yahya

As a gift from God, Zakariya was given a son named Yahya name specially chosen for this child alone. Muslim tradition narrates that Zakariya was ninety-two years old when he was told of John's birth.

In accordance with Zakariya's prayer, God made John (Yahya) renew the message of God, which had been corrupted and lost by the Israelites. As the Qur'an says:

19:7 ˹The angels announced,˺ "O Zachariah! Indeed, We give you the good news of ˹the birth of˺ a son, whose name will be John—a name We have not given to anyone before."
19:8 He wondered, "My Lord! How can I have a son when my wife is barren, and I have become extremely old?"
19:9 An angel replied, "So will it be! Your Lord says, 'It is easy for Me, just as I created you before, when you were nothing!'"
19:10 Zachariah said, "My Lord! Grant me a sign." He responded, "Your sign is that you will not ˹be able to˺ speak to people for three nights, despite being healthy."

—Surah Maryam 19:7-10

Guardian of Maryam

According to the Qur'an, Zakariya was the guardian of Maryam . The Qur'an states:

3:35 Your service, so accept it from me. You ˹alone˺ are truly the All-Hearing, All-Knowing."
3:36 When she delivered, she said, "My Lord! I have given birth to a girl,"—and Allah fully knew what she had delivered—"and the male is not like the female. I have named

her Mary, and I seek Your protection for her and her offspring from Satan, the accursed."

3:37 So her Lord accepted her graciously and blessed her with a pleasant upbringing—entrusting her to the care of Zachariah. Whenever Zachariah visited her in the sanctuary, he found her supplied with provisions. He exclaimed, "O Mary! Where did this come from?" She replied, "It is from Allah. Surely Allah provides for whoever He wills without limit."

—Surah Al Imran 3:35-37

Muslim theology maintains that Zakariya, along with John the Baptist and Jesus, ushered in a new era of prophets – all of whom came from the priestly descent of Amram (Imran), the father of the prophet Aaron. The fact that, of all the priests, it was Zakariya who was given the duty of keeping care of Mary (Maryam) shows his status as a pious man. Zakariya is frequently praised in the Qur'an as a prophet of God and righteous man. One such appraisal is in sura al-An'am:

"Likewise, ˹We guided˺ Zachariah, John, Jesus, and Elias, who were all of the righteous."

—Surah Al-An'am 6:85

After his son Yahya had been decapitated by the Children of Israel, Zakariya tried to escape from them. Some historians say that as a miracle a tree opened for Zakariya to hide in but accidentally a small part of clothing stuck out. Shaytan (Satan) saw this and took it to his advantage. He took on the form of a human and told the Children of Israel where Zakariya was hiding. For this, the soldiers then cut down the tree, killing Zakariya painfully. Some people say he was 130 years old when he died.

Shuaib

historical context

The area to which Shu'ayb was sent is named Madian in the Quran, known in English as Midian, which is frequently referenced in the Hebrew Bible. The Midianites are said to have been of Arab origin, although as neighbors of the Biblical Canaanites, they mixed with them. It is said that they were a wandering tribe, and their principal territory at the time of Musa (Moses in Islam) was the Sinai Peninsula.

Disputed identity with Jethro

Jethro is mentioned in the Bible (Exodus 3:1) as the father-in-law of Moses. Although Shu'ayb is often identified with the Midianite priest Jethro, most modern scholars reject this identification. Classical commentators such as Ibn Kathir say that Shu'ayb was the great-grandson of Abraham: It is believed that Shu'ayb was the son of Miqil, the son of Midian, the son of Abraham. This would make identification with Jethro, who lived at the time of Moses, allegedly hundreds of years after Abraham, impossible.

Claimed burial places of Shuaib

A claimed tomb of Shu'ayb is found in Jordan, 2 km (1.2 mi) west of the city of Mahis, in an area called Wadi Shu'ayb (Arabic: وَادِي شُعَيْب).

The Druze believe that the tomb of the prophet Shu'ayb is located near Hittin in the lower Galilee. Each year, on 25 April, the Druze gather at the site to discuss community matters.

There is also a tomb in the south-west of Iran (in the village of Guriyah in Shushtar) which is recorded as the tomb of Shuayb.

One of the claimed shrines of Shuaib, in Wadi Shuaib, Jordan, Levant

The Temple of Shuayb, as believed by the Druze and some Muslims, near Hittin in the Galilee

Tafsir ahsanul bayan

7:85

And We sent his brother Shuaib to Madinah (1) He said: O my people! Worship Allah, you have no deity except Him, clear proof has come to you from your Lord, after that it has been corrected, do not spread mischief, if you confirm then it is beneficial for you.

85.1 Madin was the name of the son or grandson of Hazrat Ibrahim (peace be upon him), then based on his lineage the name of the tribe was Madin and the city in which he lived also became Madin. Thus it applies to both tribe and settlement. This settlement is near Maan on the way to Hijaz. He is also referred to in another place in the Quran as Ishahab al-Ikka (inhabitant of the Bin). Hazrat Shoaib (peace be upon him) was sent to them as a prophet (see Al-Shu'ara. 176). Note: Every Prophet has been called a brother of this nation, which means a member of the same nation and tribe as Rasul Munham. In some places it is called Rasool Munham or it is also interpreted as Mannafsham, and all this means that That the messenger and prophet is a person from among the people whom Allah Almighty chooses to guide the people and through revelation. The book and the commandments have been given to him. Reveals.

85.2 After Dawat Tauheed, a big problem of weights and measures arose in this country. This mistake is also very dangerous because it reflects the moral degradation and corruption of the nation in which it occurs. Taking money in full and giving less is the biggest betrayal. That is why the news of the death of such people has been given in Surah Mutafifeen.

Swaleh

Saleh, Litt. 'the Pious'), also spelled Salih (/'sɑːlə/), is a prophet mentioned in the Quran who prophesied to the Thamud tribe in ancient Arabia, before the lifetime of the Islamic prophet Muhammad. The story of Salih is linked to the story of the she-camel of God, which was a gift given by God to the people of Thamud when they desired a miracle to confirm that Salih was indeed a prophet.

Thamud was a tribal confederation in the northwestern region of the Arabian Peninsula, mentioned in Assyrian sources during the time of Sargon II. The name of the tribe dates back to the 4th century BC. They continued to appear in documents, but by the sixth century they were considered a group that had long since become extinct.

According to the Quran, the city to which Saleh was sent was called al-Hijr, which corresponds to the Nabataean city of Hegra. The city rose to prominence as an important site in the regional caravan trade around the 1st century AD. Near the city were large, decorated rock-cut tombs that were used by members of various religious groups. [6]:146 At an unknown point in antiquity, the site was abandoned and possibly functionally replaced by Al-Ula. The site has been known as Mada'in Salih since the era of Muhammad and was named after his predecessor Salih.

Saleh is not mentioned in any historical texts or in any Abrahamic texts preceding the Quran, but the details of the destruction of Thamud may have been well known in ancient Arabia. The name of the tribe is used in ancient Arabic poetry as a metaphor for "the transience of all things".[6]:223

According to Muslim tradition, the people of Thamud were virtually dependent on Saleh for support. He was chosen by God as a messenger and sent to preach against the selfishness of the rich and to condemn the practice of shirk (idolatry or polytheism). Although Saleh preached for a sustained period of time, the people of Thamud refused to listen to his warnings and instead began asking Saleh to perform miracles for them. They said, "O Saleh! You have been among us! You have been the center of our hopes till now! Have you forbidden us from worshiping that which our fathers used to worship? But we are really about that thing Are in doubtful (restless) doubt to which You invite us."

Tafsir ahsanul bayan

11:61

And he sent their brother Saleh to the people of Thamud. You are in the earth (4) so seek forgiveness from Him and turn to Him. Undoubtedly, my Lord is near and accepting of prayers.

61.1 And there is mercy on Thamud as he was before. That means we sent Thamud. This community lived in Madain (Hijr) between Tabuk and Medina and this community came after Aad. Hazrat Saleh (peace and blessings of Allaah be upon him) was also called the brother of Samud here. Which means a member of their family and tribe.

61.2 Hazrat Saleh (peace be upon him) was also the first to invite his people to monotheism, as was the practice of the prophets.

61.3 In the beginning He created you from the earth just as your father Adam (peace be upon him) was created from clay and all human beings were created from Adam (peace be upon him) just as all human beings were created from the earth. Or it means that everything you eat comes from the earth and that food produces sperm. Which leads to human existence in the mother's womb.

61.4 That is, He created within you the ability and capacity to settle and populate the land, making you build houses to live in, cultivate food for food and work in industry and crafts to meet other necessities of life. We do.

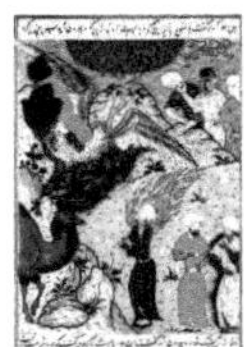

Tafsir Jalalain

11:64

And, O my people, this is the she-camel of God, a sign for you (yātan is a circumstantial qualifier operated by a demonstrative noun [Ḥadihi, 'it']). Leave him to eat on God's earth and do him no harm, hamstring [him], lest you suffer near punishment if you hamstring him.'

Tafsir Ibne Kasir

26:158

But they killed him, and then they repented. So, torture overtook them.

Their land shook with a strong earthquake and a tremendous cry echoed around them which shook their hearts from their place. Events happened to them that they did not expect, so they were left lying face down (dead) in their homes.

Tafsir Jalalain

27:52

Then their houses are [false] desolate (khwiyatn is in the reflexive because it is a circumstantial qualifier, the operator of which is the import of the demonstrative pronoun [tilaka, 'they']) because of the evil they have done, that is, their unbelief. Surely there is a sign, a lesson in it for those who have knowledge of Our power and thus receive instruction.

Asr al-Tafsir's interpretation of the words of Abu Bakr al-Jaza'iri.

7Al-Aaraf 73
Abu Bakr al-Jazairi (born 1921 AD) (died 2018 AD)

Word Explanation:
And to Thamud: That is, We were sent to Thamud, and Thamud is a tribe named after its grandfather, who is Thamud bin Aber bin Iram bin Sam bin Noah.
His brother Saleh: i.e. Saleh's name in the lineage is Saleh bin Ubaid bin Asif bin Kashah bin Ubaid bin Hazir bin Samud.

Verse: This is a sign of my sincerity that I am God's messenger to you.

And He placed you in the earth, He placed you in houses where you would like.

And you carve: you carry stones in the mountains to build houses for you to live in.

Allah Allah: The grace of Almighty God is abundant.

And do not do corruption: that is, do not spread corruption on earth, which will lead to corruption.

They were arrogant: they were arrogant, tyrannical, and arrogant, so they did not accept the truth or accept it.

meaning of verse

This is the third story of God's Prophet Saleh, peace be upon him. God Almighty said: {And to Thamud is his brother, Saleh} That is, We sent to the tribe of Thamud their brother Saleh, a prophet whom We sent with whom We sent Our messengers before him and after him, the words of the monotheism with. {He said, "O my people, worship Allah! Other than Him} And this is the meaning of the word of sincerity which was brought by the seal of the Prophet: "There is no god except God." {From your Lord to you The proof has come} It is testifying that there is no God except Him, and I am His messenger to you. This proof is a she-camel coming out of a rock in the mountain. {This is the she-camel of God to you There is a sign} A sign and any sign Believe in Almighty God who is sending me a messenger to you so that you may worship him alone and do not have any kind of association with him. So this she-camel on God's earth But leave it to eat {And do not touch it with anything bad, lest some painful torment overtake you.} So the she-camel was grazing in the meadow, and she came to the people's watering hole and drank the water. All , and it will turn into pure milk in her stomach. So they took out as much milk as they wanted, and one day he said to them, "This is a she-camel that has water, and you will get water on a known day, and she will somehow Do not harm, lest the punishment of a great day overtakes you." And the Prophet (peace and blessings of Allaah be upon him) admonished them by saying: "And remember when He made you successor after 'Aad."

John the Baptist (Yahya)

John the Baptist (c. 1st century BC – c. AD 30) was a Jewish preacher active in the region of the Jordan River in the early 1st century AD.[He is also known as John the Forerunner in Eastern Orthodoxy, some Baptist Christian traditions John the Immerser, also known as Saint John by some Catholic churches and as the Prophet Yahya in Islam. He is sometimes alternatively called John the Baptist.

Yahya ibn Zakariya literally Yahya/John, son of Zachariah), identified in English as John the Baptist, is considered a prophet and messenger of God (Allah) in Islam, sent to guide the children of I went. Israel. Muslims believe that he was a witness to God's word, announcing the arrival of Isa al-Masih (Jesus Christ).

Syrian-Egyptian Gnosticism

The Ebionites, among the early Judeo-Christian Gnostics, believed that John, along with Jesus and James the Just – whom they revered – were vegetarians.

Epiphanius of Salamis records that this group amended their Gospel of Matthew – known today as the Gospel of the Ebionites – to change what John meant to read "honey cakes" or "manna". Eats locusts.

Mandeism

John the Baptist, or Yuhanna Mbabana (lit. 'John the Baptist' Iuhanna Mababana)[] is considered to be the greatest prophet of the Mandaeans. The Mandaeans also refer to him as Yuhanna bar Zachariah (John, son of Zechariah). He plays a large role in their religious texts such as the Ginza Rabbah and the Mandaean Book of John. [The Mandaeans believe that they are directly descended from John's original disciples] but they do not believe that their religion began with John, Their beliefs trace back to their first prophet Adam.:3 According to Mandaeism, John was a great teacher, a Nasorian and a renewer of the faith.:24 John is a messenger of light (nahura) and truth (kushta).
who had the power of healing and perfect gnosis (Manda).]:48 The Mandaean texts make it abundantly clear that the early Mandaeans were extremely loyal to John and viewed him as a prophetic reformer of the ancient Mandaean/Israelite tradition. [:108 Mark Lidzbarski, Rudolf McCuch, Ethel S. Drover, Jorunn J. Scholars such as Buckley, and Sinasi Gunduz [tr] believe that the Mandaeans probably have a historical connection with the original disciples of John. The Mandaeans believe that John was married, that his wife was named Anhar, and that he had children.

Aeneasbai (Elizabeth) is mentioned as the mother of John the Baptist in chapters 18, 21, and 32 of the Mandaean book of John.

Tafsir ahsanul bayan

19:12

Hey Yahaya! Hold fast to My Book (1) and We gave him wisdom from his youth (2).

12.1 That is, Allah gave Yahya Alaihissalam to Hazrat Zakaria Alaihissalam and when he grew up, although he was still a child, Allah ordered him to hold the Book firmly i.e. to walk on it. , The book refers to the Torah or any book that has been specifically revealed to those we do not know about.

12.2 Hukm refers to knowledge, wisdom, consciousness, understanding of the rules of religion written in the book, comprehensiveness of knowledge and action, or prophecy. Imam Shuqani says that there is no objection in including all these things in the order.

Asr al-Tafsir's interpretation of the words of Abu Bakr al-Jaza'iri.

19 Mary 15
Abu Bakr al-Jazairi (born 1921 AD) (died 2018 AD)

Word Explanation:
How can I have a son?: That is, in what way can I have a son?
Aatiya: That means it dried up my joints and bones.
Aya: What signs indicate that my wife is pregnant?

Together: That is, the state of being of good character makes you mute.
From mihrab: the prayer area in which one prays, which is the mosque.
So He revealed to them: He pointed out to them, and pointed out to them.
And We gave him wisdom when he was a child: Judgment and wisdom have the same meaning, and they are the knowledge of the secrets of jurisprudence and Shariah in religion.
Our compassion is from ourselves: that is, the kindness we extend to people.
Zakat: Means purification from sins and misdeeds.
Oppressive and disobedient: That is, arrogant and not accepting the truth, disobedient and disobeying the command of Almighty God and the command of one's parents.
And peace be upon him: that is, his protection from the devil who harmed him on the day he was born, his protection from the destruction of the grave on the day he dies, and from the greatest terror on the day he is resurrected alive. His safety. ,
Meaning of the verse:
Great context remains in mentioning God's mercy upon his servant Zechariah. When his Lord Almighty gave him good news about Yahya, he said: What did Lord Almighty reveal to him about him: In any direction, the boy will come to me safely from a woman other than my own, from him a mother, but she gives me the strength to have intercourse with her and enable her to conceive, for as you know, O my Lord, I have

reached such an age that my bones and joints wither. Are, and it is very strong, like my wife is barren and will not have a child. Then the Blessed and Most High Jehovah answered him as the Almighty had said: {He said thus} That is, the matter is as you said, O Zechariah, but {Your Lord said, "It is easy for Me" meaning you To give birth to a child is easy and simple, without any difficulty, despite your weakness and old age and your wife being barren, and He gives you the sign that I {and I created you before, and you were nothing. } Just as your God was able to create you when you were nothing, He is able to give you a child despite your weakness and the barrenness of your wife. Here, Zechariah asked his God to make him a sign that would indicate to him the time of his wife's pregnancy. Child, then he said what Almighty God had said to him: {And I created you first, and you were nothing}. He said, "My Lord, make a sign for me." He said, "Your sign is that you should not speak to people for three nights. He is of healthy body, neither dumb nor sick that prevents him from speaking. And some Mihrab } i.e., the place of prayer in which he prays {so He revealed them} i.e., he nodded and pointed towards them { praising God in the morning and evening, i.e. remembering God by praying and praising at both these times to do. Here he came to know about his wife's pregnancy, for her abstinence from speaking while her body and senses remain intact is a sign of the onset of pregnancy, and the Almighty says: {O Yahya, take the scripture with strength} That is Lord Almighty said this to the boy after he reaches the age of three years. Almighty God ordered him to learn the Torah and work on it with diligent strength and determination, and His word {and We gave him knowledge. M as a boy, that is, We gave him the understanding of the Book and the knowledge of the secrets of Sharia law when he was a boy who had not yet reached the age of puberty.

Jesus Christ (Isa)

Jesus' childhood home is identified in the gospels of Luke and Matthew as the town of Nazareth in Galilee, where he lived with his family. Although Joseph appears in the description of Jesus' childhood, there is no further mention of him. [better source needed] Other members of his family—his mother, Mary, his brothers James, Joses (or Joseph), Judas and Simon, and his unnamed sisters—are mentioned in the Gospels and other sources.[In the Gospel of James Jesus' maternal grandparents are Joachim and Anne. The Gospel of Luke records that Mary was a relative of Elizabeth, the mother of John the Baptist. Contemporary extra-biblical sources consider Jesus and John the Baptist to be second cousins, with the belief that Elizabeth was the daughter of Anne's sister Sobey.

The Gospel of Mark reports that early in his ministry, Jesus comes into conflict with his neighbors and family. Jesus' mother and brothers come to take him away because people are saying he is crazy. Jesus replied that his followers were his true family. In the Gospel of John, Jesus and his mother attend a wedding in Cana, where he performs his first miracle at her request. Later, she follows him to the crucifixion, and he expresses concern over her well-being.

In Mark 6:3 Jesus is called τέκτων (tekton), a term traditionally understood to mean carpenters, but can also refer to makers of objects in various materials, including builders.

The Gospels indicate that Jesus could read, interpret, and debate scripture, but this does not mean that he received formal Scriptural training.
The Gospel of Luke describes two visits by Jesus and his parents to Jerusalem during his childhood. They come to the temple in Jerusalem to present Jesus as an infant according to Jewish law, where a man named Simeon prophesies about Jesus and Mary. When Jesus, at the age of twelve, goes missing on a pilgrimage to Jerusalem for Passover, his parents find him sitting among the teachers in the temple, listening to them and

asking questions, and the people are surprised by his understanding and answers. Are surprised by. Mary scolds Jesus for being missing, to which Jesus replies that he "must be at his Father's house".

In the Synoptics, Jesus teaches extensively, often in parables, about the Kingdom of God (or, in Matthew, the Kingdom of Heaven). The kingdom is described as both imminent and already present in the ministry of Jesus. Jesus promises to include in the Kingdom those who accept his message.[He speaks of the "Son of man," an apocalyptic figure who will come to gather the chosen people.

Jesus tells people to repent of their sins and surrender themselves completely to God. He tells his followers to observe Jewish law, although some believe that he himself broke the law, for example regarding the Sabbath. When asked what the greatest commandment was, Jesus answered: "You shall love the Lord your God with all your heart, and with all your soul, and with all your mind... and another one is like it: ' You must love your God." "Your equal neighbor." Other moral teachings of Jesus include loving your enemies, abstaining from hatred and lust, turning the other cheek, and forgiving those who have sinned against you.

The Gospel of John presents Jesus' teachings not simply as his own preaching, but as divine revelation. John the Baptist, for example, says in John 3:34: "He whom God has sent speaks the words of God, for he gives the Spirit without measure." Jesus says in John 7:16, "My teaching is not my own, but that of him who sent me." He emphasizes the same point in John 14:10: "Do you not believe that I am in the Father, and the Father is in me? The words that I speak to you, I do not speak on my own, but the Father who is in me. I keep doing his work."

The approximately 30 parables constitute about one-third of Jesus' recorded teachings.[Parables appear in longer sermons and in other places in the narrative. They often contain symbolism, and they usually connect the physical world with the spiritual world. Common themes in these stories include God's kindness and generosity and the dangers of crime. [Some of His parables, such as the Prodigal Son,[are relatively simple, while others, such as the growing seed, are sophisticated, profound, and profound.[When His disciples asked Him why He spoke to people in parables, Jesus answered that the chosen disciples are given to "know the mysteries of the kingdom of heaven", unlike the rest of them, "For whoever has will have, more will be given and he will have abundance. But whoever has If not he will be even more deprived", adding that most people of his generation have become "dull-hearted" and thus unable to understand.
Jesus cleansing a leper, medieval mosaic from Monreale Cathedral, late 12th to mid-13th century

In the gospel accounts, Jesus devoted a large part of his ministry to performing miracles, especially healings. Miracles can be classified into two main categories: healing miracles and nature miracles. Miracles of healing include healing of physical ailments, exorcisms, and resurrection of the dead. Miracles of nature reflect the power of Jesus over nature, and include turning water into wine, walking on water, and calming a storm, etc. Jesus says that his miracles are from a divine source. When His opponents suddenly accused Him of performing exorcisms by the power of Beelzebul, the prince of demons, Jesus retorted that He did so by "the Spirit of God" (Matthew 12:28) or by "the finger of God." Do this, arguing that all logic suggests that Satan will not allow his demons to aid God's children because it would divide Satan's house and bring his kingdom to ruin; Furthermore, he asks his adversaries if he is exorcized by Beelzebub, "By whom do your sons drive them out?" In Matthew 12:31-32, he says that while all kinds of sins, "even offenses against God" or "offenses against the Son of man", will be forgiven, whoever does good (or "holy soul") will never be forgiven; They always carry the blame of their sins.

In John, Jesus' miracles are described as "signs", which were performed to prove his mission and divinity. In the Synoptics, when asked by some teachers of the law and some Pharisees to give miraculous signs to prove his authority, Jesus refused, [208] saying that any sign other than the sign of the prophet Jonah would be corrupt. And will not come near bad people. Furthermore, in the Synoptic Gospels, crowds regularly react with astonishment to Jesus' miracles and pressure him to heal their sick. In the Gospel of John, Jesus is presented as free from crowd pressure, who often respond to his miracles with faith and belief. A characteristic shared among all of Jesus' miracles in the gospel accounts is that he performed them freely and never requested or accepted any form of payment. Gospel passages that include descriptions of Jesus' miracles often also include teachings, and the miracles themselves include an element of teaching. Many miracles teach the importance of faith. For example, in the purification of the ten lepers and the raising up of Jairus' daughter, the beneficiaries are told that their healing was due to their faith.[

After the life of Jesus, his followers, as described in the first chapter of the Acts of the Apostles, were all Jews either by birth or by conversion, for which the Biblical term "conversion" is used, and historians refer to them as Is referred to as. Jewish Christian. The initial gospel message was spread orally, probably in Aramaic, but almost immediately also in Greek. The New Testament's Acts of the Apostles and the Epistle to the Galatians record that the first Christian community was centered in Jerusalem and that its leaders included Peter, James, the brother of Jesus, and John the Apostle.

After his conversion, the Apostle Paul spread the teachings of Jesus to various non-Jewish communities in the Eastern Mediterranean. It is said that Paul's influence on Christian thinking is more significant than that of any other New Testament author.

By the end of the first century, Christianity became recognized internally and externally as a separate religion from Judaism, which was refined and developed in the centuries after the destruction of the Second Temple.

Several quotations in the New Testament and other Christian writings of the first centuries indicate that early Christians generally used and respected the Hebrew Bible (Tanakh) as a religious text, mostly in Greek (Septuagint) or Aramaic (Targum).) in translations. ,

<u>Early Christians</u> wrote many religious works, including works included in the New Testament canon. The canonical texts, which have become the main sources used by historians trying to understand the historical Jesus and the sacred texts within Christianity, were probably written between 50 and 120 AD.
The teachings of Jesus and retellings of his life story have significantly influenced the course of human history, and have directly or indirectly influenced the lives of billions of people, even non-Christians. He is considered by many to be the most influential person of all time, having found significant place in many cultural contexts.

Apart from his own disciples and followers, Jews of Jesus' time generally rejected him as the Messiah, as does Judaism today. Christian theologians, ecumenical councils, reformers, and others have written extensively about Jesus over the centuries. Christian denominations have often been defined or characterized by their descriptions of Jesus. Meanwhile, Manichaeans, Gnostics, Muslims, Druze, the Bahá'í Faith, and others have found a prominent place for Jesus in their religions.

Tafsir Ibne Kasir

4:171

Preventing the People of the Book from going to extremes in religion

Allah says;

See more

O people of the Scripture! Do not cross the limits in your religion,

Allah forbids the people of the scriptures from going to extremes in religion, which is a common characteristic of them, especially among Christians.

Christians exaggerated Jesus until they raised him above the level that Allah had given him. They raised him above the rank of prophet and made him a deity, whom they worshiped in the same way as they worshiped Allah.

He exaggerated even more in the case of those he claimed were his followers, claiming that they were inspired, thus following every word he said whether it was true or not. Wrong, whether it is guidance or misguidance, truth or falsehood.

They accepted their rabbis and monks as their masters besides Allah. (9:31)

Imam Ahmad recorded that Ibn Abbas said that Umar said that the Messenger of Allah said,

Do not praise Me unnecessarily like the Christians do with exaggerated words about Jesus, son of Mary. Really, I am a slave, so say,

Servant of Allah and His messenger.

This is the word of Al-Bukhari.

Imam Ahmad recorded that Anas bin Malik said that;

A man once said, "O Muhammad! You are our master and the son of our master, the most righteous of us and the son of the most righteous of us..." The Messenger of Allah said,

Hey people! Say what you want, but don't let the devil deceive you.

I am Muhammad bin Abdullah, servant and messenger of Allah. I swear to Allah! I don't like you raising me above the position that Allah has given me.

Allah's statement,

(Nor say anything about Allah other than the truth.) That is, do not lie and do not claim that Allah has a wife or a son, Allah is more pure than what they ascribe to Him. Glory, praise and honor be to Allah in His power, majesty and greatness, and there is no deity or god worthy of worship except Him.

Allah said;

Al-Masih 'Isa, son of Mary, was (nothing else) a messenger of Allah and His Word, which He gave to Mary and (from her) the soul;

Jesus is only one of Allah's servants and one of His creatures. Allah said to him, 'Be', and it came to be, and He sent him as a messenger.

Jesus had a word from Allah which he gave to Mary,

That is, He created it with the word 'B' which He sent to Mary along with Gabriel. With the permission of Allah, Jibril breathed the life of Jesus into Mary, and as a result Jesus came into existence.

This incident was in place of normal pregnancy between a man and a woman, which results in the birth of a child. That is why 'Isa was a Word and Ruh (Soul) created by Allah, because He had no father to conceive Him. Rather, He came into existence through the word that Allah said, 'Be', and He came into existence through the life that Allah sent with Jibril.

Allah said,

Al-Masih ('Isa), son of Mary, was nothing more than a messenger; There were many such messengers who passed away before him. His mother was (Mariam) Siddiqa. Both of them ate food. (5:75)

And Allah said,

In fact, in the sight of Allah the image of Jesus is the image of Adam. He created him from dust, then (He) said to him, "Be! - And it was. (3:59)

And he who guarded his purity, We breathed into him (the garment) and We made him and his son ('Isa) a sign for all those who go forth. (21:91)

and Maryam, Imran's daughter who protected her chastity. (66:12)

And Allah said about Christ,

He (Jesus) was no more than a servant. We bestowed our blessings upon him. (43:59)

Meaning of "His Word and a Spirit from Him"
Abdur-Razzaq narrated that the uncle said that Qatada said the ayah,
Christian denomination
Saeed bin Batriq, the Patriarch of Alexandria and a renowned Christian scholar, noted four hundred years after the Hijrah that;
During the reign of Constantine a Christian council was convened, which gave the city its name. At this council, what Christians called the Great Trust unfolded, which is actually the Great Betrayal. There were more than two thousand patriarchs in this council and they were so disorganized that they got divided into many sects, in which some sects had twenty, fifty or a hundred members etc.

When the king saw that there were more than three hundred patriarchs who held similar views, he agreed with them and adopted their sect.
Constantine – who was a heretical philosopher – gave his support to this sect, out of respect for which, churches were built and doctrines were taught to young children who were baptized on this sect, and books were written about it. Meanwhile, the king oppressed all other sects.

Another council created the sect called the Jacobites, while the Nestorians were formed at the third council.
All three sects agreed that 'Jesus was divine', but there was controversy over the way in which Jesus' divinity related to his humanity; Were they in unity or did Allah incarnate in Jesus?
These three sects accuse each other of heresy and we believe that all three are unbelievers.

An-Nisa' 4:171

English - Footnote (Hilali)

Ruh-ullah: According to the early religious scholars from among the Companions of the Prophet (ﷺ) and their students and the Mujtahidun, there is a rule to distinguish between the two nouns in the genitive construction:

a) When one of the two nouns is Allah, and the other is a person or a thing, e.g. Allah's House (Bait-ullah); Allah's Messenger (Rasul-ullah); and Allah's slave ('Abdullah); Allah's spirit (Ruh-ullah), the rule for the above words is that the second noun, e.g., house, messenger, slave or spirit is created by Allah and is honourable in His Sight, and similarly, Allah's spirit may be understood as the spirit of Allah, in fact it is a soul created by Allah, i.e. 'Isa (Jesus). And it was His Word: "Be!"- and he was [i.e. 'Isa (Jesus) was created like Adam].

b) But when one of the two is Allah and the second is neither a person nor a thing, then it is not a created thing but is a Quality of Allah, e.g. Allah's Knowledge ('Ilm-ullah); Allah's Life (Hayat-ullah); Allah's Statement (Kalam-ullah); and Allah's Self (Dhat-ullah).

Narrated 'Ubadah [radhi-yAllahu 'anhu]: The Prophet (ﷺ) said, "If anyone testifies that La ilaha illallah (none has the right to be worshipped but Allah Alone) Who has no partners, and that Muhammad (ﷺ) is His slave and His Messenger, and that Jesus ['alayhis-salam] is Allah's slave and His Messenger and His Word ("Be!" -- and he was) which He bestowed on Mary and a spirit (Ruh) created by Him, and that Paradise is the truth, and Hell is the truth -- Allah will admit him into Paradise with the deeds which he had done even if those deeds were few." (Junadah, the subnarrator said, "'Ubadah added: 'Such a person can enter Paradise through any of its eight gates he likes.' ") [Sahih Al-Bukhari, 4/3435 (O.P.644)]

Az-Zukhruf 43:63

English - Tafsir Jalalayn

And when Jesus came with the clear signs, the miracles and the prescriptions [of the Law], he said, 'Verily I have brought you wisdom, prophethood and the prescriptions of the Gospel, and [I have come] to make clear to you some of what you are at variance over, in the way of the rulings of the Torah for what concerns religion and otherwise -- and he [indeed] made clear to them the matters of religion. So fear God and obey me.

Tanwir al-Mikbas min Tafsir Ibn Abbas

43 Az-Zukhruf 66
Wait if they do not turn away from their claims (in nothing) except the coming of the hour, (that it will come upon them suddenly, when they do not know) when they have no idea of the punishment that will come upon them?
Tafsir Ibn Abbas, trans. Mocren Guizhou
Royal Al-Bayt Institute for Islamic Thought, Amman, Jordan.
Asr al-Tafsir's interpretation of the words of Abu Bakr al-Jazairi,

43 Decoration 65
Abu Bakr al-Jazairi (born 1921 AD) (died 2018 AD)
Word Explanation:
And when Jesus came with clear proofs: that is, when Jesus, the son of Mary, came to the Children of Israel with miracles and the law.
He said, "I have brought you wisdom." That is, he said to the children of Israel, "I have brought you prophecy and gospel laws."
And I have come to make you understand what you disagree about, that is, I have come to make you understand what you disagreed about regarding the laws of the Torah regarding religion and other things.

So fear God and obey: that is, fear God and obey what He has revealed to you regarding God's commands and prohibitions.

Verily, God is my God and your God, so worship Him: That is, God is my God and your God, so worship Him with love, glory and devotion to Him.

It is the straight path: that is, fearing God, obeying the Messenger and worshiping God as He has revealed, Islam is expressed as the straight path.

There was a difference of opinion among them in the parties: namely, as to Jesus, is He God: or the Son of God, or the third of three?

So from the torment of the Day of Sorrow, woe to those who persecuted: that is, woe to those who told lies and falsehood about Jesus.

Are they just waiting for the moment to come suddenly without them realizing it? That is, despite standing firm on what they said about Jesus, what these parties are waiting for is the hour that will come to them suddenly, while they do not understand?

Meaning of the verse:

After Almighty God mentioned His joy over the dispute of the polytheists in Mecca and the lies told by Ibn al-Zabari about the angels, Uzayr and Jesus, peace be upon them, that they are in Hell with those who followed them. used to worship, God Almighty rejected the angels, Almighty and Jesus because he did not order people to worship them until they were held accountable, but instead ordered their worship to be the devil, so Satan and those who worship him. Dwelling in hell, and mentioned the honor and status of Almighty God Jesus and said that he was a servant whom He provided a prophet and made him an example to the Children of Israel by which they could prove the power of Almighty God , For He created him without a father just as He created Adam without father or mother, but He created him from dust. He referred to the message of Jesus, peace be upon him, to the Children of Israel so that it would be a warning to the infidels of Mecca. Then Almighty God said, "And when Jesus came with clear proofs, that is, He came to the Children of Israel with clear proofs, which are the gospel and miracles such as raising the dead, healing the blind and lepers, and Similarly, He said to them, 'I have come to you with knowledge, that is, prophecy from God, and explained to you some of the rules of the Torah and those matters in which you disagree. So O Children of Israel, fear God, That is, fear the punishment resulting from his crimes, and obey the commands and prohibitions that I have informed you from God

Almighty. Verily, God is my Lord and your Lord, that is, my Lord and your Lord. There is no god except Him. No, so worship Him by showing love towards Him and by renouncing His anger because of love for Him, His glory, fear of Him, and...

Tafsir ahsanul bayan

4:157

And thus to say, "We killed Jesus, the messenger of God, Jesus son of Mary, although they neither killed him nor crucified him (1) but created for them an image of him (Jesus) (2) Be assured that those who disagree about Jesus (peace be upon them) are in doubt about Him, they have no certainty about Him except guessing (3) That much is certain. That they did not kill them.

157.1 This makes it clear that the Jews succeeded in killing Jesus, not in crucifying him. As he had planned. (As in the margin of verse 55 of Surah Al-Imran)

The brief description is over.
157.2 This means that when Jesus (peace be upon him) came to know about the conspiracy of the Jews, he gathered his disciples, who were 12 or 17 in number, and said, "Those of you in my place Who should be killed?" Ready? So that by Allah Almighty, his appearance may be made like mine.

A young man prepared for this. So Jesus was taken from there to heaven. Later the Jews came and took that young man and crucified him. Who was made to look like Jesus (peace be upon him). The Jews continued to think that we had crucified Jesus, while Jesus was not there at that time, he was taken to heaven with a living body (Ibn Kathir and Fath al-Qadir).

157.3 After the murder of Jesus' lookalike, one group continued to say that Jesus was murdered, while another group realized that the crucified man was not Jesus; some people say that they also saw Jesus going to heaven. Saw it happen. To God). The Malakaniya faction stated that this murder and crucifixion occurred entirely from the viewpoint of both Nasut and theology (Fath al-Qadir), however, they remained subject to disagreement and hesitation and doubt.

Hazrat Muhammad Sallahu Alaihi WaSallam

Muhammad[was an Arab religious, social and political leader and the founder of Islam. According to Islamic doctrine, he was a prophet divinely inspired to preach and confirm the monotheistic teachings of Adam, Abraham, Moses, Jesus, and other prophets. He is believed to be the seal of the prophets within Islam, with his teachings and practices, along with the Quran, forming the basis of Islamic religious belief.

Muhammad was born in Mecca around 570 AD. He was the son of Abdullah ibn Abd al-Muttalib and Amina bint Wahb. His father, Abdullah, the son of the Quraysh tribal leader Abd al-Muttalib ibn Hashim, died a few months before Muhammad's birth. His mother Amina died when he was six years old, leaving Muhammad an orphan. He was raised under the care of his grandfather, Abd al-Muttalib, and uncle, Abu Talib. In his later years, he would periodically seclude himself in a mountain cave called Hira for several nights of prayer. When he was 40 years old, around 610 BC, Muhammad reported being visited by Gabriel in the cave and receiving his first revelation from God. In 613, Muhammad began to preach these revelations publicly, declaring that "God is one", that complete "surrender" (Islam) to God (Allah) is the right way of life (deen). , and he was a prophet and messenger of God like the other prophets of Islam.

Muhammad's followers were initially few in number, and experienced hostility from the polytheists of Mecca for 13 years. To escape ongoing persecution, he sent some of his followers to Abyssinia in 615, before he and his followers later moved from Mecca to Medina (then known as Yathrib) in 622. This event, Hijra, marks the beginning of the Islamic calendar, also known as the Hijri calendar. In Medina, Muhammad united the tribes under the Constitution of Medina. In December 629, after eight years of intermittent fighting with the Meccan tribes, Muhammad gathered an army of 10,000 Muslim converts and marched on the city of Mecca. The conquest was largely unopposed and Muhammad captured the city with little bloodshed. In 632, a few months after returning from a farewell pilgrimage, he fell ill and died. By the time of his death, most of the people of the Arabian Peninsula had converted to Islam.

The revelations (each known as an ayah – literally, "signs [of God]") that Muhammad reported receiving until his death are composed of verses of the Quran, which are interpreted by Muslims verbatim as "God It is considered to be the word on which the religion is based. In addition to the Quran, the teachings and practices (Sunnah) of Muhammad found in the Hadith and Sira (biographical) literature are also preserved and used as sources of Islamic law.

Muhammad began praying alone for several weeks each year in a cave called Hira on Mount Jabal al-Nour, near Mecca. According to Islamic tradition, in 610 AD, when he was 40 years old, the angel Gabriel appeared to him during a visit to the cave. The angel showed him a cloth with verses from the Quran and instructed him to read it. When Muhammad admitted his illiteracy, Gabriel strangled him hard, almost suffocating him, and repeated the order. As Muhammad reiterated his inability to read, Gabriel strangled him again in the same manner. This sequence occurred once more before Gabriel finally recited the verses, helping Muhammad memorize them. These verses later became Quran 96:1-5.

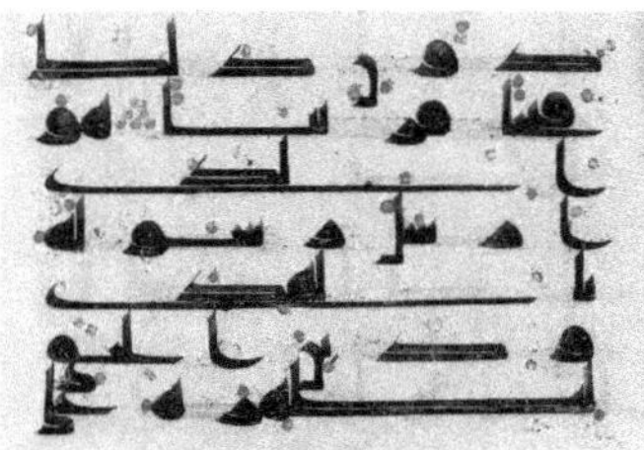

This experience horrified Muhammad, but he was quickly reassured by his wife Khadija and his Christian cousin Warqa ibn Nawfal. Khadija instructed Muhammad to tell her if Gabriel returned. When he appeared during their private time, Khadija tested Muhammad by sitting on his left thigh, right thigh, and lap, and interrogated Muhammad whether the creature was present each time. When Khadija took off her clothes with Muhammad in her arms, she reported that Gabriel left at that very moment. Khadija thus asked him to be happy as she concluded that it was not a devil but an angel who had come to visit her.

Muhammad's conduct during moments of inspiration often led his contemporaries to allege that he was under the influence of a jinn, a prophet, or a sorcerer, which suggests that his experiences during these events were widely recognized in antiquity. The data obtained were similar to the experiences related to this. Arab. Nonetheless, these mystical seizure events may serve as persuasive evidence to his followers regarding the divine origin of his revelations. Some historians believe that the graphic descriptions of Muhammad's condition in these examples are probably genuine, as it is impossible for them to have been fabricated by later Muslims.

Shortly after Warqa's death, revelations ceased for a period of time, causing Muhammad to become deeply distressed and have suicidal thoughts. [g] On one occasion, he reportedly climbed a mountain with the intention of jumping off. However, upon reaching the climax, Gabriel appeared to him and confirmed his status as the true messenger of God. This encounter pacified Muhammad and he returned home. Later, when there was another long interval between revelations, he repeated this action, but Gabriel intervened in the same way, calming him and forcing him to return home.

Muhammad was confident that he could separate his thoughts from these messages. Early Quranic revelations used methods of warning non-believers of divine punishment, while promising rewards to believers. He told of possible consequences such as famine and murder for those who rejected Muhammad's God and hinted at past and future disasters. The text also emphasized the impending final judgment and the threat of hell fire for skeptics. According to Muslim tradition, Muhammad's wife Khadija was the first to believe that he was a prophet. He was followed by Muhammad's ten-year-old cousin Ali ibn Abi Talib, close friend Abu Bakr, and adopted son Zayd.

Asr al-Tafsir's interpretation of the words of Abu Bakr al-Jaza'iri.

53 Star 11
Abu Bakr al-Jazairi (born 1921 AD) (died 2018 AD)

Word Explanation:
And when the star sets: that is, when it rises and sets, then the Pleiades.

Your friend has not gone astray: that is, Muhammad, God bless him and grant him peace, has strayed from the path of guidance.

And one who has been misled: that is, one who is veiled in error, who is based on ignorance based on corrupted belief.

And whatever He says is of His own volition, that is, whatever He says about Almighty God does not come of His own volition.

It is nothing other than a revelation that has been revealed: that is, it is nothing other than a divine revelation that has been revealed to Him.

He was taught by a very powerful angel: That is, he was taught by a very powerful angel, Gabriel, peace be upon him.

Dhul-Murrah: That is, for the soundness of his body and mind, and thus he had great strength.

Therefore he settled when he was on the highest horizon: that is, he settled when he was on the horizon at the time of the rising of the sun in the image in which God had created him. The Prophet, may God's prayers and peace be upon him, saw that he and he were accompanied by horses that blocked the horizon towards the west. It was the Prophet, may God's prayers and peace be upon him, who asked Gabriel to show him himself in the image in which God had created him. on that.

Then he came closer and hung: That is, he came near her and hung, that is, he increased the closeness.

So it was around the corner: that is, it was near, around the corner, that is, the amount of two arcs.
So he revealed to his servant what he had revealed: that is, God Almighty revealed to his servant Gabriel what Gabriel had revealed to the Prophet, may God bless him and give him peace.

The heart did not lie about what it saw: That is, the heart of the Prophet did not lie about what it saw when it saw the image of Gabriel, peace be upon him.

Do you dispute with him about what he sees? That is, O polytheists, do you dispute with him about what he sees of the image of Gabriel?

And he saw him a second time: that is, in his image, again in the sky on the night of his captivity.

In Sidra al-Muntaha: Which is a buckthorn tree on the right side of the throne, which no angel can cross.

There is a heaven of refuge: that is, the angels and the souls of the martyrs and the saints, the saints of God, take refuge there.

When the Sidr is covered by what it covers: that is, by the Light of God Almighty, by what it covers.

The vision neither deviated nor went astray: that is, Muhammad's vision neither turned to the right nor to the left, nor did it go beyond the limits that were set for it.

He saw one of the greatest signs of his Lord: namely, he saw Gabriel in his form and saw a green flap that blocked the horizon of the sky.

Meaning of the verse:

The saying of Almighty God, "And the star," upon His saying, "among the greatest signs of their Lord," confirms the prophethood of Muhammad, His servant and messenger, may God bless him and grant him peace. He swore by the star when it descended, and by the star of the Pleiades when it disappeared from the horizon, that Muhammad, the companions of the Quraysh who had been with him since his birth, had never deviated from them. She was not absent from him for a period of more than forty years, so she was a perfect companion. They have not strayed from the path of guidance, and they know it. He was not tempted by any temptation, nor did he wear the cloak of ignorance in words or actions, so he was led astray by it.

My another books

Sr no.	Book
1	World's Major religions, doctrines and sects
2	An introduction to the Holy Qur'an and it's unsolved mysteries
3	How did humans and language originate ?
4	Islam an introduction and sect
5	Sermons of great people
6	Prayer
7	Allah an introduction
8	Is Al khizr still alive today?
9	Story of harut and marut
10	Grief
11	The mysterious story of Al kahf (Ar raqim)
12	Naming of God
13	Who was sheeba?
14	Death concept of the Holy Qur'an
15	Where is peace?
16	Origin of ancient religious book, it's author and original copy

All these books are available in Hindi language and other international languages and are also available in e-book for free on Google Play Store.

All books available on

notionpress.com

My personal introduction

My name is Abdul Waheed, my father's name is Late Haji Ubaidur Rahman and mother's name is Jaibunnisa. I have liked scientific ideology since childhood and have a calm nature and attachment to books. Due to which my curiosity interest has been continuously used in new discoveries and information. I got selected in polytechnic while doing BSc, but unfortunately it remained incomplete because father and brother died.

Two words of my father, which are very precious for my life,

first - earn honestly, do not take support of lies,

secondly, respect food and eat as much as you want. That's why the education remained incomplete due to the responsibility of the house, then later getting married. Still did not lose courage and today the book is available in front of you in the form of my thoughts. If any information is left incomplete, please let us know.

Thank you .

Contact-

Abdul Waheed, Barabanki, Uttar Pradesh, India (BHARAT)

https://www.facebook.com/profile.php?id=100091298026218